"Can I do anything to help you?"

Ava touched his arm again, this time lightly, brushing her fingertips across the slick material of his jacket.

The human contact and the emotion behind it made him shiver. Max clenched his teeth. "You can't do anything to help. You've done enough."

She grabbed the door handle and swung open the door before the car even stopped.

"Hold on. I'll walk you up."

"I thought you were anxious to get rid of me."

He didn't want to leave Ava, but he had to—for her own safety. "I was anxious to get you away from the lab and back home. The police can pick it up from here."

He followed her to the front door. She dragged her keys from her purse and slid one into the dead bolt. It clicked and she opened the door.

Apprehension slithered down his spine and he held out a hand. "Wait."

But it was too late. Ava had stepped across the threshold and now faced two men training weapons on her.

And this time she wasn't behind bulletproof glass.

UNDER FIRE

CAROL ERICSON

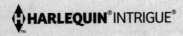

To Marilyn, for all that you do.

Recycling programs
for this product may
not exist in your area.

ISBN-13: 978-0-373-74897-6

Under Fire

Copyright © 2015 by Carol Ericson

Printed in U.S.A.

HARLEQUIN®
www.Harlequin.com

Carol Ericson lives with her husband and two sons in Southern California, home of state-of-the-art cosmetic surgery, wild freeway chases and a million amazing stories. These stories, along with hordes of virile men and feisty women, clamor for release from Carol's head. It makes for some interesting headaches until she sets them free to fulfill their destinies and her readers' fantasies. To learn more about Carol, please visit her website, carolericson.com, "Where romance flirts with danger."

Books by Carol Ericson

HARLEQUIN INTRIGUE

Brothers in Arms: Retribution series

Under Fire

Brody Law series

The Bridge
The District
The Wharf
The Hill

Brothers in Arms: Fully Engaged series

Run, Hide
Conceal, Protect
Trap, Secure
Catch, Release

Guardians of Coral Cove series

Obsession
Eyewitness
Intuition
Deception

Visit the Author Profile page at Harlequin.com for more titles.

CAST OF CHARACTERS

Max Duvall—A covert ops agent wired to kill, he's now fighting to regain his soul and humanity, and he's in danger of destroying the one woman who can help him reclaim both.

Ava Whitman—A disgraced doctor who discovers she's been aiding and abetting the enemy vows to redeem herself, and she's going to start with a damaged, sexy undercover ops agent who will give his life for her...if he doesn't kill her first.

Simon Skinner—This agent starts a chain of events that will destroy him and put those he loves in danger.

Dr. Charles Arnoff—A mad scientist who will do anything to test his wild theories, even if it means creating a cadre of agents bent on destruction.

Cody Whitman—Ava's flaky brother has gotten her in deep trouble before, but this time he just might end up saving his sister—and the world.

Adrian Bessler—An agent on the run, will he join forces with Max and Ava, or is he still working with the enemy?

Caliban—The mysterious leader of Tempest—the black ops organization that's trying to throw world affairs into chaos—wants to rule the world and satisfy his vendetta against Jack Coburn and Prospero in the process.

Chapter One

The shell casings from the bullets pinged off the metal file cabinets. One landed inches from her nose and rolled one way and then the other, its gold plating winking at her under the fluorescent lights. The acrid smell of gunpowder tickled her nostrils. She smashed her nose against the linoleum to halt the sneeze threatening to explode and give away her position.

Someone grunted. Someone screamed. Again.

Ava held her breath as the rubber sole of a black shoe squeaked past her face. She followed its path until her gaze collided with Dr. Arnoff's.

From beneath the desk across from her, he put his finger to his lips. His thick glasses, one lens crushed, lay just out of his reach between the two desks. With his other finger, he pointed past her toward the lab.

Afraid to move even a centimeter, Ava blinked her eyes to indicate her understanding. If they could make their way to the lab behind the bulletproof glass and industrial-strength locks they might have a chance to survive this lunacy.

The shooter moved past the desks, firing another round from his automatic weapon. Glass shattered—not the bulletproof kind. A loud bump, followed by a crack and the door to the clinic, her domain, crashed open.

Greg bellowed, "No, no, no!"

Another round of fire and Greg's life ended in a thump and a gurgle.

Ava squeezed her eyes closed, and her lips mumbled silent words. *Keep going. Keep going.*

If the shooter kept walking through the clinic, he'd wind up on the other side in the waiting room. At this time of night, nobody was in the waiting room, which led to a door and a set of stairs to the outside.

Keep going.

He returned. His boots crunched through the glass. Then he howled like a wounded animal, and the hair on the back of Ava's neck stood at attention and quivered.

The footsteps stopped on the other side of the desk—her pathetic hiding place. In the sudden silence of the room, her heartbeat thundered. Surely he could hear it, too.

He kicked at a shard of glass, which skittered between the two desks.

Ava turned widened eyes on Dr. Arnoff and

swallowed. She harbored no hopes that the doctor could take down the shooter. Although a big man, his fighting days were behind him. Their best hope was to make it to the lab and wait for help.

The black-booted foot stepped between the desks, smashing the other lens of Dr. Arnoff's glasses. A second later the shooter lifted the desk by one edge and hurled it against the wall as if it were a piece of furniture in a dollhouse.

Exposed, Dr. Arnoff scrambled for cover, his army crawl no match for the lethal weapon pointed at him. The bullets hit his body, making it jump and twitch.

Ava dug a fist against her mouth, and her teeth cut into her lips. The metallic taste of her blood mimicked the smell permeating the air.

Then her own cover disappeared, snatched away by some towering hulk. She didn't scream. She didn't beg. The gunman existed in a haze behind the weapon that he now had aimed at her head.

His gloved finger on the trigger of the assault rifle mesmerized her. She mumbled a prayer with parched lips. *Click.* She sucked in a breath. *Click.* She gritted her teeth.

Click. He'd run out of ammo.

He reached into the pocket of his fatigues, and adrenaline surged through her body. She clambered over the discarded desk and launched herself at the lab door. With shaking hands she scrabbled for the badge around her neck and pressed it to the reader. The red light mocked her.

Her badge didn't allow her access to this lab. Her exclusion from the lab had been a source of irritation to her for almost two years. How could she forget that now?

She dropped to her knees and crawled to Dr. Arnoff's dead body. Her fingers trembled as she unclipped the badge from the pocket of his white coat.

Amid the clicking and clacking behind her, the gunman muttered to himself.

Expecting another round of shots at any second, Ava swiped Dr. Arnoff's badge across the reader. The green lights blinked in a row as if she'd just won a jackpot. She had.

She yanked open the heavy door and shoved it closed just as the shooter looked up from his task. Five seconds later, a volley of bullets thwacked the glass.

Knowing the gunman could lift a badge from any of the dead bodies around him just as she had, Ava slid three dead bolts across the door and took two steps back.

This windowless room, clicking and buzzing with machinery, computers and refrigeration, offered no escape, but it did contain a land-line telephone. Maybe someone had been able to make a call to the police when the mayhem started, but no cavalry had arrived to the rescue yet.

After his first round, the crazed man outside her sanctuary had stopped shooting. He seemed to be searching the bodies of her fallen coworkers—looking for a badge, no doubt. He wouldn't find Dr. Arnoff's.

Ava pounced on the receiver of the telephone on the wall beside the door. Her heart skipped a beat. No dial tone. She tapped the phone over and over, but it remained dead.

Even if she had her cell phone, which remained in the pocket of her lab coat hanging on a hook in the clinic, it wouldn't do any good. Nobody could get reception in this underground building in the middle of the desert.

The lock clicked and she spun around. The shooter was leaning against the door, pressing a badge up to the reader. The lock on the handle responded, but the dead bolts held the door securely in place.

She'd resented being locked out of this lab, but now she couldn't be happier about those extra reinforcements.

He grabbed the handle and shook it while releasing another roar.

Ava covered her galloping heart with one hand as she studied the glittering eyes visible from the slits in the ski mask. What did he want? Drugs? Why murder all these people for drugs? Why come all the way out here to a high-level security facility to steal meds?

He gave up on the door and shook his head once. Then he reached up and yanked the ski mask from his head.

Ava gasped and stumbled back. She knew him. Simon. He was one of her patients, one of the covert agents the lab treated and monitored.

Guess they hadn't monitored him closely enough.

"Simon?" She flattened her palm against the glass of the window. "Simon, put down your weapon. The police are on their way."

She had no idea if the police were on their way or not. The lab used its own security force, so she and her coworkers never had a reason to call in the police from the small town ten miles away in this New Mexico desert. Since the lab's security guards had made no attempt to stop Simon, she had a sick feeling Simon had already dealt with them.

"You need help, Simon. I can help you." She licked her lips. "Whatever you need me to say to the authorities, I'll say it. We can tell them it was your job, the stress."

His mouth twisted and he lunged at the window, jabbing the butt of his gun against the glass, which shivered under the assault.

Ava blinked and jerked back. She made a half turn and scanned the lab. If he somehow made it through the door and she got close enough to him, she could stick him with a needle full of tranquilizer that would drop him in his tracks. She could throw boiling water or a chemical mixture in his face.

He'd never let her get that close. He'd come through shooting, and she wouldn't have a chance against those bullets. None of the others had. She gulped back a sob.

The bullets started again. Simon had stepped away from the door and continued spraying bullets at the glass. That window hadn't been designed to withstand this kind of relentless barrage. She knew. She'd asked when she started working here, curious about the extra security of this room.

He knew it, too. Sweat beaded on Simon's ruddy face as he took a breather. He didn't even need to reload. He rolled his shoulders as if preparing for the long haul.

Then he resumed firing at the window.

Again, Ava searched the room, tilting her head back to examine the ceiling. Unfortunately, the ceiling was solid, except for one vent. She eyed the rectangular cover. Could she squeeze through there?

Simon took another break to examine the battered window, placing his weapon on the floor beside him.

She tried to catch his gaze, tried to make some human contact, but this person was just a shell of the Simon she had known. The sarcastic redhead who did killer impressions had disappeared, replaced by this creature with dead eyes.

Ava's breath hitched in her throat. Beyond Simon, a figure decked out in black riot gear loomed in the doorway of the clinic. Was it someone from security? The police?

Not wanting to alert Simon, she inched farther away from the window and kept her gaze glued to Simon's face.

The man at the door yelled, "Simon!"

How did he know who the shooter was? Had someone from the lab seen Simon before the rampage started and reported him?

Simon turned slowly.

"Give it up, Simon." The man raised his weapon. "We can get help, together."

Simon growled and swayed from side to side.

Would he go for his gun on the floor?

Taking a single step into the room, the man tried again. "Step away from your weapon, Simon. We'll figure this out."

Simon shouted, "They have to pay!"

Ava hugged herself as a chill snaked up her spine. His animalistic sounds had frightened her, but his words struck cold fear into her heart. Pay for what? He'd gone insane, and they'd been responsible for him, for his well-being.

"Not Dr. Whitman. It's not her fault."

Ava threw out a hand and grasped the edge of a counter to steady herself. Her rescuer knew her name? His voice, bellowing from across the room, muffled by the mask on his face, still held a note of familiarity to her. He must be one of the security guards.

"It is." Simon stopped swaying. "It *is* her fault."

He dropped to the floor and jumped up, clutching his weapon. He raised it to his shoulder but it didn't get that far.

The man from across the room fired. Simon spun around and fell against the window, which finally cracked.

Ava clapped a hand over her mouth as she met Simon's blue stare. The film over his eyes cleared. They widened for a second and he gasped. Blood gurgled from his gaping mouth. He slid to the floor, out of her sight.

Every muscle in her body seized up and she couldn't move.

The security guard kept his weapon at his

shoulder as he stalked across the room. When he reached the window of the lab, he pointed his gun at the floor, presumably at Simon.

Ava covered her ears, but the gunfire had finally ceased.

Slinging his weapon over his shoulder, the man gestured to the door. "Open up. It's okay now."

Would it ever be okay? She'd just watched a crazed gunman, one of her patients, mow down her coworkers and had barely escaped death herself.

She stumbled toward the door and reached for the first lock with stiff hands. It took her several tries before she could slide all the dead bolts. Then she pressed down on the handle to open the door.

The man, smelling of gunpowder and leather and power, stepped into the lab. "Are you okay, Dr. Whitman?"

She knew that voice but couldn't place it. Tilting her head, she cleared her throat. "I—I'm not physically hurt."

"Good." His head swiveled back and forth, taking in the small lab. "Are there any blue pills in this room?"

She took a step back from his overpowering presence. "Blue pills? What are you talking about?"

"The blue pills." He stepped around her and yanked open a drawer. "I need as many blue pills as you have in here—all of them."

"I don't know what you mean." She blinked and edged toward the door. Had she just gone from one kind of crazy to another? Maybe this man was Simon's accomplice and they were both after drugs.

He continued his search through the lab, repeating his request for blue pills, pulling out drawers and banging cupboard doors open.

A crash from another area of the building made them both jump, and he swore.

Taking her arm in his gloved hand, he said, "We need to get out of here unless you can tell me where to find some blue pills."

"I told you, I don't know about any blue pills, and there's no serum on hand either." Maybe he was after the vitamin boost the agents received quarterly.

He grunted. "Then let's go."

"Wait a minute." She shook him off. "H-he's dead, right? Simon's dead?"

The man nodded once.

"Then why do we have to leave? Maybe that noise was the police breaking in here." Cold fear flooded her veins and she hugged her body. "Are there more? Is there another gunman?"

"He's the only one."

"Then I'd rather stay here and wait for the rest of your—" she waved a hand at him "—security force or the cops or whoever is on the way. That could be them."

He adjusted his bulletproof vest and took her arm again. "We don't want to wait for anyone."

Confusion clashed with anger at his peremptory tone and the way he kept grabbing her. She jerked her arm away from him and dug her heels into the floor. "Hold on. My entire department has just been murdered. I was almost killed. I'm not going anywhere. I don't even know who the hell you are."

"Sure you do." He reached up with one hand and yanked the ski mask from his head.

Her eyebrows shot up. Max Duvall. Another one of her patients, another agent—just like Simon.

"Y-you, you're…"

"That's right, and you're coming with me. Now." He scooped her up with one arm and threw her over his shoulder. "Whether you want to or not."

Chapter Two

"Let me go!" She struggled and kicked her legs, but Dr. Ava Whitman was a tiny thing.

He could get her to go with him willingly if he sat down and explained the whole situation, but they didn't have time for that. That could be Tempest at the door right now. He couldn't even risk doing a more thorough search for the blue pills. He'd have to just take her at her word that there were none at the lab.

Maybe Dr. Whitman already knew the whole situation. Knew why Simon had gone postal. He couldn't trust anyone…not even pretty Dr. Whitman.

Clamping her thighs against his shoulder, he stepped over the dead bodies littering the floor. When he navigated around the final murder victim in his path at the door of the clinic, Dr. Whitman stopped struggling and slumped against his back. If she'd had her eyes open the whole way, she probably just got her fill of blood and guts.

He crossed through the waiting room and kicked open the door to the stairwell. He slid Dr. Whitman down his body so that she was facing him, his arm cinched around her waist.

"Will you come with me now? I need you to walk up these stairs and out the side door. I have a car waiting there."

Through his vest, he could feel the wild beat of her heart as it banged against her chest. "Where are we going? Why can't we wait here for the police?"

"It's not safe." He grabbed her shoulders and squeezed. "Do you believe me?"

Her green eyes grew round, taking up half her face. She glanced past him at the clinic door and nodded. Then she grabbed the straps on his bulletproof vest. "My purse, my phone."

"Are they in the clinic?"

"Yes."

He shoved back through the door and pulled her along with him. He didn't quite trust that she wouldn't go running all over the lab searching for the security guards. Wouldn't do her any good anyway—Simon had killed them all.

She broke away from him and yanked her purse from a rack two feet from the body of a coworker. She dipped her hand in the pocket of her lab coat hanging on the rack and pulled out a phone.

Another crash erupted from somewhere in the building, and Dr. Whitman dropped her phone. It skittered and twirled across the floor, coming to a stop at the edge of a puddle of blood.

She gasped and hugged her purse to her chest.

The noise, closer than the previous one, sent a new wave of adrenaline coursing through his veins. "Let's go!"

Her feet seemed rooted to the floor, so he crossed the room in two steps and curled his fingers around her wrist, tugging her forward. "We need to leave."

Still holding on to Dr. Whitman, Max plucked her phone from the floor and headed toward the stairwell again. He half prodded, half carried Dr. Whitman upstairs, and when they reached the door to the outside, he inched it open, pressing his eye to the crack.

The car he'd stolen waited in the darkness. He pushed open the door of the building and a blast of air peppered with sand needled his face. He ducked and put an arm around Dr. Whitman as he hustled her to the vehicle.

She hesitated when he opened the passenger door. The wind whipped her hair across her face, hiding her expression.

It was probably one of shock. Or was it fear? "Get in, Dr. Whitman. They're here."

This time she didn't even ask for clarification.

His words had her scrambling into the passenger seat.

He blew out a breath and lifted the bulletproof vest over his head. Would Simon have turned the gun on him after everything they'd gone through together? Sure he would've. That man in there who'd just committed mass murder bore no resemblance to the Simon he knew.

He threw the vest in the backseat and cranked on the engine. He floored the accelerator and went out the way he came in—through a downed chain-link fence.

He hit the desert highway and ten minutes later blew past the small town that served the needs of the lab. The lab didn't have any needs now.

After several minutes of silence, Dr. Whitman cleared her throat. "Are we going to the police now? Calling the CIA?"

"Neither."

Her fingers curled around the edge of the seat. "Where are we going?"

"I'm taking you home."

"Home?" She blinked her long lashes. "Whose home?"

Without turning his head, he raised one eyebrow. "Your home. You have one, don't you? I know you don't live at the lab—at least not full-time."

"Albuquerque. I live in Albuquerque."

"I figured that. Once I drop you off, you're free to call whomever you like."

"But not now?"

"Not as long as I'm with you."

She bolted upright and wedged her hands against the dashboard. "Why? Don't you want to meet with the CIA? Your own agency? Tell them what happened back there?"

"What do *you* think happened back there?" He squinted into the blackness and hit his high beams.

"Simon Skinner lost it. He went on a murderous rampage and killed my coworkers, my friends." She stifled a sob with the back of her hand.

She showed real grief, but was the shock feigned? Extending his arms, he gripped the steering wheel. "How much do you know about the work you do at the lab?"

"That's a crazy question. It's my workplace. I've been there for almost two years."

"Your job is to treat and monitor a special set of patients, correct?"

"Since you're one of those patients, you should know." She dragged her fingers through her wavy, dark hair and clasped it at the nape of her neck.

One soft strand curled against her pale cheek.

Whenever he'd seen her for appointments, her hair had been confined to a bun or ponytail. Now loosened and wild, it was as pretty as he'd imagined it would be.

"And the injections you gave us, the vitamin boost? Did you work on that formula?"

She jerked her head toward him and the rest of her curls tumbled across her shoulder. "No. Dr. Arnoff developed that before I arrived."

"Did he tell you what was in it?"

"Of course he did. I wouldn't inject my patients with some mystery substance."

"Were you allowed to test it yourself? Did you work in that lab?"

"N-no." She clasped her hands between her bouncing knees. "I wasn't allowed in the lab."

"Why not? You're a doctor, aren't you?"

"I…I'm… The lab requires top secret clearance. I have secret clearance only, but Dr. Arnoff showed me the formula, showed me the tests."

He slid a glance at her stiff frame and pale face. Was she still in shock over the events at the lab or was she lying?

"Now it's your turn."

His eyes locked onto hers in the darkness of the car. "What do you mean?"

"It's your turn to answer my questions. What were you doing at the lab? You weren't scheduled for another month or so. Why can't we call the police or the CIA, or Prospero, the agency you work for?"

"Prospero?"

She flicked her fingers in the air. "You don't have to pretend with me. Nobody ever told me the name of the covert ops agency we were supporting, but I heard whispers."

"What other whispers did you hear?" A muscle twitched in his jaw.

"Wait a minute." She smacked the dashboard with her palms. "I thought it was your turn to answer the questions. What were you doing there? Why can't we call the police?"

"You should be glad I was there or Skinner would've gotten to you, too."

Folding her arms across her stomach, she slumped in her seat, all signs of outrage gone. She made a squeaking noise like a mouse caught in a trap, and something like guilt needled the back of his neck.

He rolled his shoulders, trying to ease out the tension that had become his constant companion. "I was at the lab because I found out Skinner was going to be there. We can't call the police for obvious reasons. I'm deep undercover. I don't want to stand around and explain my presence to the cops."

"And your own agency? Prospero?"

"Yeah, Prospero." If Dr. Whitman wanted to

believe he worked for Prospero, why disappoint her? The less she knew the better, and it sounded as if she didn't know much—or she was a really good liar. "I'll call them on my own. I wanted to get you out of there in case there was more danger on the way."

"You seemed convinced there was."

"We were in the middle of the desert, in the middle of the night at a top secret location with a bunch of dead bodies. I didn't think it was wise for either of us to stick around."

She leaned her head against the window. "What should I do when I get home?"

He drummed his thumbs against the steering wheel. If Tempest and Dr. Arnoff had kept Dr. Whitman in the dark, she should be safe. Tempest would do the cleanup and probably resume operations elsewhere—with or without Dr. Ava Whitman.

"Once I drop you off and hit the road, you can call the police." He frowned and squinted at the road. "Or do you have a different protocol to follow?"

She turned a pair of wide eyes on him. "For this situation? We had no protocol in place for an active shooter like that."

Maybe the whole bunch of them out there, including Dr. Arnoff, were clueless. No, not

Arnoff. He had to have known what was going on, even if he didn't know the why.

"Then I guess it's the cops." Even though the local cops would never get to the whole truth. He pointed to the lights glowing up ahead. "We're heading into the city. Can you give me directions to your place? Is there someone at home?"

She hadn't touched her cell phone once since they escaped from the lab. Wouldn't she want to notify her husband? Boyfriend? Family?

"I live alone."

He supposed she'd want to be with someone, have someone comfort her. God knew, he wasn't capable. "Do you have any family nearby? Any friends to stay with?"

"I don't have any family…here. I'm kind of new to the area and I spend a lot of time at the lab, so I haven't had much time to cultivate friends."

Hadn't she told him she'd been working at the lab for two years? Two years wasn't enough time to make friends? Maybe she'd been taking some of her own medicine.

"When the police come, they may want to take you back to the scene. You'll probably have to lead them to the facility."

She gasped and grabbed his arm. "What do I tell them about you?"

He stiffened and glanced down at her hand gripping the material of his jacket. She dropped it.

Was she offering to cover for him? He figured she'd waste no time at all blabbing to the cops about the man who'd shot Skinner and then whisked her out of the lab. "Tell them the truth."

No law enforcement agency would ever be able to track him down anyway. Tempest had made sure of that.

"I can always tell them you were a stranger to me, that you wouldn't tell me your name." Her fingers twisted in her lap as she hunched forward in her seat.

She *was* offering to cover for him. Why would she do that, unless she knew more than she'd pretended to know?

"You'd lie for me?"

She jerked back and whipped her head around. "Lie? You're an agent with a government covert ops team. If I learned anything at the lab, it was how to keep secrets. I never revealed any of my patients' names to anyone, and I'm not about to start now."

"I appreciate the…concern." He lifted a shoulder. "Tell the cops whatever you like. I'll be long gone either way."

She tilted her chin toward the highway sign. "That's my exit in five miles."

"Then I'll deliver you safe and sound to your home, Dr. Whitman."

"You can call me Ava."

After riding in silence for a while, Ava dragged her purse from the floor of the car into her lap and hugged it to her chest. "What happened to Simon? He looked...dead inside."

"He snapped." His belly coiled into knots. If Simon could snap like that, he could snap, too.

"Did you know about his condition somehow?"

"I had an idea, and when I discovered he was heading out to New Mexico I put two and two together."

"Was it the stress of the assignments? I saw most of you four times a year, but of course you weren't allowed to discuss anything with me. You all seemed well-adjusted though."

Max snorted. "Yeah, I guess some would call that well-adjusted."

"You weren't? You're not? Can I do anything to help you?"

She touched his arm again, this time lightly, brushing her fingertips across the slick material of his jacket.

The human contact and the emotion behind it made him shiver. He clenched his teeth. "You can't do anything to help...Ava. You've done enough."

She snatched her hand back again and studied her fingernails. "This is the exit."

He steered the car toward the off-ramp and eased his foot off the accelerator. She continued giving him directions until they left the desert behind them and rolled into civilization.

He pulled in front of a small house with a light glowing somewhere inside.

She grabbed the door handle and swung open the door before the car even stopped.

"Hold on. I'll walk you up."

"I thought you were anxious to get rid of me."

He scratched the stubble on his chin. That hour-long drive had been the closest he'd come to normalcy in a long time. He didn't want to leave Ava, but he had to—for her own safety.

"I was anxious to get you away from the lab and back home. The police can pick it up from here."

If there was anything left of the lab when they got there. Tempest had to know by now that one of its agents had gone off the rails. The crashes and noises at the lab could've been Tempest.

"Well, here I am." She spread her arms.

He jingled the keys in his palm and felt for his handgun and other gear on his belt as he followed her to the front door.

She dragged her own keys from her purse and

slid one into the dead bolt. It clicked and she opened the door.

Apprehension slithered down his spine, and he held out a hand. "Wait."

But it was too late.

Ava had stepped across the threshold and now faced two men training weapons on her.

And this time she wasn't behind bullet-proof glass.

Chapter Three

Simon was back—in stereo. Ava caught a glimpse of two men with guns pointed at her for a split second before Max snatched her from behind, lifting her off her feet and jerking her to the side.

At the same instant, she heard a pop and squeezed her eyes closed. If the men had shot Max, she was finished.

An acrid smell invaded her nostrils and she opened her lids—and regretted it immediately. The black smoke pouring from her front door stung her eyes and burned her throat.

"Hold your breath. Close your eyes." Max lifted her and tucked her under one arm as if she were a rag doll.

She felt like a rag doll. The jolt of fear that had spiked her body when she saw the gunmen had dissipated into a curious out-of-body sensation. A creeping lethargy had invaded her limbs, which now dangled uselessly, occasionally banging against Max's body.

If she was lethargic, Max was anything but. His body felt like a well-oiled machine as he sprinted for the car, still clutching her under one arm. He loaded her into the front seat and seconds later the car lurched forward with a shrill squeal.

"Get your seat belt on."

Her hand dropped to the side of the seat, but her fingers wouldn't obey the commands of her fuzzy brain. At the next sharp turn, she fell to the side, her head bumping against the window.

A vise cinched her wrist. "Snap out of it, Ava! I need you."

How had Max known that those three little words amounted to a rallying cry for the former Dr. Ava Whitman?

She rubbed her stinging eyes. She sniffled and dragged a hand beneath her nose. She coughed. She grabbed her seat belt and snapped it into place.

Without taking his eyes from the road, Max asked, "You okay?"

She ran her hands down her arms as if wondering for the first time if she'd been shot. "I'm fine. Did they shoot at us? How did they miss… unless…?"

"I'm okay. They didn't get a shot off."

"I thought—What was all that smoke? The noise?"

"I was able to toss an exploding device at

them before they could react. I don't think they were expecting you to have company."

"Let me get this straight." She covered her still-sensitive eyes with one hand. "Two men had guns pointed at us when we walked through the door and you were able to pull me out of harm's way and throw some smoke bomb into the house at the same time?"

"I had the advantage of surprise."

Her hand dropped to her throat. "Did you know someone would be there waiting? Because I was sure surprised to see them standing there."

"Let's just say I had a premonition."

She shook her head. "Superhuman."

Max jerked the steering wheel and the car veered to the right. "Why'd you say that?"

She tilted her head. Why the defensiveness?

"When I saw those guns, I thought we were both dead. Somehow you got us out of there alive. Did I ever thank you? Did I ever thank you for what you did at the lab?"

"Not necessary." He flexed his fingers.

"Are you going to tell me what those men were doing at my house? Are they with Simon? Did they come to finish the job he started?"

She held her breath. If she had a bunch of covert ops agents after her, what was her percentage of survival? Especially once Max Duvall left her side, and he would leave her side—they always did.

"I'm not sure, Ava."

The name sounded tentative on his lips for a man so sure of himself. Agent Max Duvall had always been her favorite patient and it had nothing to do with his dark good looks or his killer body—they all had those killer bodies.

Most of the agents were hard, unfriendly. Some wouldn't even reveal their names. Max always had a smile for her. Always asked about her welfare, made small talk. She looked forward to the quarterly visits by Max—and Simon.

Smashing a fist against her lips, she swallowed a sob. Simon had been friendly, too. He'd even admitted to her that he was engaged, although such personal communications from the agents were verboten. Where was Simon's fiancée now?

Did Max have a wife or a girlfriend sitting at home worried about him, too?

"Are you sure you're okay?"

She blinked and met Max's gaze. They were back on the desolate highway through the desert, and Max's eyes gleamed in the darkness. A trickle of fear dripped down her back. Maybe those men back at her house were there to save her from Max. Maybe Max and Simon were in league together.

"Are you afraid of me?" His low, soft voice floated toward her in the cramped space of the car.

"N-no." She pinned her aching shoulders back against the seat. "No, I'm not. You saved my life—twice. I'm just confused. I have crazy thoughts running through my head. Do you blame me?"

"Not at all."

"If you could tell me what's going on, I'd feel better—as much as I can after tonight's events. I deserve to know. Someone, something is out to extinguish my life. I need to know who or what so I can protect myself."

"I'll protect you."

"From what? For how long?" Her fingers dug into the hard muscle of his thigh. "You have to give me more, Max. You can't keep me in the dark and expect me to trust you. I can't trust like that—not anymore."

Tears blurred her vision, and she covered her face with her hands. Hadn't he just told her to snap out of it? If she wanted to prove that she deserved the hard truth, she'd have to buck up and quit with the waterworks.

"You're right, Ava, but I have a problem with trust, too. I don't have any."

"You don't think you can trust me?" Her voice squeaked on the last syllable.

"You worked in that lab."

"The lab that you visited four times a year. The lab that kept you safe. The lab that treated your injuries—both physical and mental. The lab that made sure you were at your peak performance levels so you could do your job, a job vital to the security of our country."

"Stop!" He slammed his palms against the steering wheel, and she shrank against her side of the car.

"That lab, that bastion of goodwill and patriotic fervor, turned me into a mindless, soulless machine." He jabbed a finger in her face. "You did that to me, and now you have as much to fear from me as you did from Simon. I'm a killer."

Chapter Four

Icy fingers gripped the back of Ava's neck and she hunched her shoulders, making herself small against the car door. She shot a side glance at Max. The glow from the car's display highlighted the sharp planes of his face, lending credence to his declaration that he was a machine. But a killer? He'd saved her—twice. Unless he'd saved her for some other nefarious purpose.

Her fingers curled around the door handle, and she tensed her muscles.

Her movement broke his trancelike stare out the windshield. Blinking, he peeled one hand from the steering wheel and ran it through his dark hair.

"I—I won't hurt you, Dr. Whitman."

She whispered, "Ava."

He cranked his head to the side, and the stark lines on his face softened. "Where can I take you…Ava?"

She jerked forward in her seat. She couldn't

go home, as if she'd ever called that small bungalow teetering at the edge of the desert home.

But if Max thought he could launch a bombshell at her like that and then blithely drop her off somewhere, he needed to reprogram himself.

Had he really just blamed her for Simon's breakdown?

"Before you take me anywhere—" she pressed her palms against her bouncing knees "—you're going to explain yourself. How is any of this my fault?"

He squeezed his eyes closed briefly and pinched the bridge of his nose. "I shouldn't have yelled, but I don't know if I can trust you."

"Me?" She jabbed an index finger at her chest. "You don't know if you can trust me? You're the one who whisked me away from the lab, led me into an ambush and then threatened to kill me."

He sucked in a sharp breath. "That wasn't a threat. I don't make threats."

His words hung in the space between them, their meaning clear. This man would strike without warning and without mercy. The fact that she still sat beside him, living and breathing, attested to the fact that despite his misgivings he must trust her at least a little bit.

"You warned me that you were a killer, like Simon."

"What exactly do you think the agents of… Prospero do if not kill?"

"You kill when it's necessary. You kill to protect the country. You kill in self-defense."

"Is that what you think Simon was doing?"

She stuffed her hands beneath her thighs. "No, but that's what you were doing when you took him out."

He nodded once and his jaw hardened again. "I won't hurt you, Ava."

She swallowed. His repetition of the phrase sent a spiral of fear down her spine. Was he trying to convince her or convince himself?

"Tell me where I can drop you off, and you'll be fine. Friends? Family?"

"I told you, I don't have any friends or family in this area." She pushed the hair from her face in a sharp gesture, suddenly angry at him for forcing her to admit that pathetic truth.

"I can take you to an airport and get you on a plane to anywhere."

"No." She shook her head and her hair whipped across her face again. "Before I get on a plane to anywhere, I want you to explain yourself. What happened to Simon? Why did you blame me? Why did Simon attack the lab?"

"If you don't know, it's not safe for me to tell you."

"Bull." She jerked her thumb over her shoulder. "Those two men were waiting for me at my house. I wasn't safe back there, and I'm not safe now. What you tell is not going to make it any worse than it already is. And you know that."

Lights twinkled ahead, and she realized they'd circled back into the city after a detour on a desert highway so that he could make sure they hadn't been followed.

He pointed to a sign with an airplane on it. "I can take you straight to the airport and buy you a ticket back home to your family. You can contact the CIA and tell them what happened. The agency will help you."

"But the agency is not going to tell me what's going on. I want to know. I deserve to know after you accused me of being complicit in Simon's breakdown."

"You were."

She smacked her hands on the dashboard. "Stop saying that. This is what I mean. You can't throw around accusations like that without backing them up."

He aimed the car for the next exit and left the highway. "It's going to be morning soon. Let's get off the road, get some rest. I'll tell you everything, and then you're getting on that plane."

She sat quietly as Max followed the signs to the airport. He turned onto a boulevard lined with airport hotels and rolled into the parking lot of a midrange highrise, anonymous and nondescript.

He dragged a bag from the trunk of the car and left the keys with the valet parking attendant.

She hadn't realized how exhausted she was until they walked through the empty lobby of the hotel.

A front desk clerk jumped up from behind the counter. "Do you need a room?"

"Yeah." Max reached for the back pocket of his camouflage pants. Without the bulletproof vest, the black jacket and the ski mask, he looked almost normal. Could the hotel clerk feel the waves of tension vibrating off Max's body? Did he notice the tight set of Max's jaw? The way his dark eyes seemed to take in everything around him with a single glance? *Normal* was not a word she'd use to describe Max Duvall.

"Credit card?"

"We don't use one. Filed for bankruptcy not too long ago." Max offered up a tight smile along with a stack of bills. "We'll pay cash for one night."

The clerk's brow furrowed. "The problem is if you use anything from the minibar or watch a movie in the room, we have no way to charge you."

Max thumbed through the money and shoved

it across the counter. "Add an extra hundred for incidentals."

The clerk's frown never left his face, but he seemed compelled to acquiesce to Max. She didn't blame him. Max was the type of man others obeyed.

Five minutes later, Max pushed open the door of their hotel room, holding it open for her.

She eyed the two double beds in the room and placed her purse on the floor next to one of them. If the clerk downstairs had found the request for two beds odd, he'd put on his best poker face. Maybe he'd figured their *bankruptcy* had put a strain on the marriage.

She perched on the edge of the bed, knees and feet primly together, watching Max pace the room like a jungle cat.

He stopped at the window and shifted to the side, leaning one shoulder against the glass.

"Do you want something from the minibar? Water, soft drink, something harder?"

She narrowed her eyes. She hadn't expected him to play host. Despite rescuing her from mortal danger, he hadn't seemed too concerned with her well-being. He'd gone through the motions and had acknowledged her shock and fear, but he'd done next to nothing to comfort her. Because he still didn't trust her.

"I'll have some water." She pushed up from

the bed and hovered over the fridge on the console. "Do you want something?"

"Soda, something with caffeine."

The man didn't need caffeine. He needed a stiff drink, something to take off the hard edges.

She swung open the door of the pint-size fridge and plucked a bottle of water from the shelf. She pinched the neck of a wine bottle and held it up. "You sure you don't want some wine?"

"Just the soda, but I don't mind if you want to imbibe. You could probably use something to relax you."

"That's funny." She placed the wine on the credenza and grabbed a can of cola from the inside door of the fridge. "I was just thinking you needed something to relax *you*."

"Relax?"

He blinked his eyes and looked momentarily lost, as if the idea of relaxation had never occurred to him.

"Never mind." She crossed the room and held out the can to him.

When he took it, his fingers brushed hers and she almost dropped the drink. That was the first time he'd touched her without grabbing, gripping and yanking. Although she'd touched him before, plenty of times.

Like all of the agents, his body was in prime condition—his muscles hard, his belly flat, barely concealed power humming beneath the smooth skin. As a medical professional, she'd always maintained her distance but she couldn't deny she'd looked forward to Max Duvall's appointment times.

But that was then.

She planted her feet on the carpet, widening her stance in front of him. "Are you going to tell me what this is all about now? Why did Simon go on a murderous rampage, why is someone out to get me, and why did you blame it all on me?"

He snapped the tab on his can and took a long pull from it, eyeing her above the rim. "Let's sit down. You must be exhausted."

"I am, but not too exhausted to hear the truth." She walked backward away from him and swiveled toward the bed, dropping onto the mattress. She had to hold herself upright because out of Max's tension-filled sphere, she did feel exhausted. She felt like collapsing on the bed and pulling the covers over her head.

He dragged a chair out from the desk by the window and sat down, stretching his long legs in front of him. It was the closest he'd come to a relaxed pose since he'd stormed into the lab in full riot gear.

"What do you know about the work at the lab?"

"Didn't we go through this already? We support a covert ops agency, Prospero, by monitoring and treating its agents. Part of the lab is responsible for developing vitamin formulas that enhance strength, alertness and even intelligence."

"But you're not part of that lab."

"N-no. I'm the people doctor, not the research doctor."

He slumped in his chair and took another gulp of his drink. "How do you know you support Prospero? Isn't that supposed to be classified information? After all, the general public knows nothing of Prospero...or other covert ops agencies under the umbrella of the CIA."

"We're not supposed to know, but like I said, people talk." She waved her hand in the air. "I've heard things around the lab."

"You heard wrong."

She choked on the sip of water she'd just swallowed. "I beg your pardon?"

"The rumor mill had the wrong info or it purposely spread the wrong info. You don't support Prospero. You support another covert ops team—Tempest."

"Oh." Clearing her throat, she shrugged. "One agency or the other. It doesn't make any difference to me. They must be related groups, since both of their names come from the Shakespeare play."

He nodded slowly and traced the edge of the can with his fingertip. "They are related, in a way."

"So what difference does it make whether we supported Prospero or Tempest?"

"I said the agencies were related, not the same. One is a force for good, and the other..." His hand wrapped around the can and his knuckles grew white as he squeezed it.

The knots in her stomach twisted with the aluminum. "Tempest is a force for evil? Is that what you mean?"

"Yes."

She jerked the hand holding the bottle and the water sloshed against the plastic. "That's ridiculous. I wouldn't work for an agency like that. Would you? You're a Tempest agent. Are you telling me you all signed up for service knowing Tempest had bad intentions?"

"Not knowingly. Did you? How *did* you come to work at the lab?"

Unease churned in her gut and a flash of heat claimed her flesh from head to toe.

"What is it?" Max hunched forward, bracing his forearms against his thighs.

"Dr. Arnoff recruited me." She pressed her fingers to her warm cheeks. "He gave me the job because I had nowhere else to go."

"Why not, Ava?" His dark eyes burned into her very soul.

"I—I had lost my license to practice medicine. I was finished as a physician before I had even started. Dr. Arnoff gave me a chance. He gave me a chance to be a doctor again." Her voice broke and she took a gulp of water to wash down the tears.

"Why? What happened? You're a good doctor, Ava."

His gentle tone and kind words had the tears pricking the backs of her eyes.

She sniffed. "I'm not a doctor. I made a mistake. Someone betrayed me, but it was my own fault. I was too trusting, too stupid."

He opened his mouth and then snapped it shut. Running a hand through his thick, dark hair until it stood up, he heaved a sigh. "So, Arnoff took advantage of your situation, your desperation to get you to work for Tempest."

"And you? Simon? The others? How did Tempest recruit you?"

He dropped his lashes and held himself so still, she thought he'd fallen asleep for a few seconds. When he opened his eyes, he seemed very far away. "You're not the only one who has made mistakes, Ava."

"So, what is Tempest? What do they do? Wh-what have you done for them?"

A muscle twitched in his jaw, and he ran his knuckles across the dark stubble there. "Tempest is responsible for assassinations, kidnappings, tampering with elections around the world."

"I'm not naive, Max. A lot of covert ops groups are responsible for the same types of missions."

"Tempest is different. An agency like Prospero may commit acts of espionage and violence, but those acts promote a greater good—a safer world."

She crossed her arms and hunched her shoulders. "And what does Tempest promote?"

Max's dark eyes burned as he gazed past her, his nostrils flaring. He seemed to come to some decision as his gaze shifted back to her face, his eyes locking onto hers.

"Terror, chaos, destruction."

"No!" A sharp pain drilled the back of her skull and she bounded from the bed. "I don't believe you. That turns everything we did in that lab, all our efforts, into a big lie. My coworkers were good people. We were doing good work there. We were protecting agents who were protecting our country."

He lunged from his chair, slicing his hand through the air, and she stumbled backward as he loomed over her, his lean frame taut and menacing.

"Tempest agents do not protect this country.

Tempest is loyal to no one country or group of nations. Tempest is loyal to itself and the shadowy figure that runs it."

Her knees shook so much she had to grip the edge of the credenza. Despite Max's sudden burst of fury, she didn't fear him. The man had saved her twice. But she did fear his words.

Maybe he was delusional. Maybe this was how Simon had started. Maybe she *should* fear Max Duvall.

"I don't understand." The words came out as a whisper even though that hadn't been her intent. She had no more control over her voice than she did the terror galloping throughout her body.

He ran both hands through his hair, digging his fingers into his scalp. "I don't see how I can be any plainer. Tempest is a deep undercover agency, so rogue the CIA is completely in the dark about its operations and methods. Tempest carries out assassinations and nation building all on its own, and these interests do not serve the US or world peace."

"Then what is their purpose?"

As if realizing his close proximity to her for the first time, Max shuffled back, retreating to the window, wedging a shoulder against the glass.

"I don't know. Tempest's overall goal is a mystery to me."

"If Tempest is so evil, why are you one of its agents? You said you were recruited, but why'd you stay? There's no way the agency could keep you in the dark, not...not like me."

She held her breath, bracing for another outburst. Instead, Max relaxed his rigid stance. His broad shoulders slumped and he massaged the back of his neck.

"You really have no idea, do you? You haven't figured it out yet."

A muscle beneath her eye jumped, and she smoothed her hands across her face. She sipped in a few short breaths, pushing back against the creeping dread invading her lungs.

"Why should I know? You haven't explained that part to me. You've made some crazy, wild accusations, throwing puzzle pieces at me, expecting me to fit them together when I haven't even processed the mass murder I just witnessed."

Her knees finally buckled and she grabbed for the credenza as she sank to the carpet.

Max's long stride ate up the distance between them, and he placed a steadying hand on her shoulder. "Are you okay? We should've saved this conversation for morning, after some sleep and some food."

When she didn't respond, he nudged her. "Can you stand up?"

She nodded, but the muscles in her legs refused to obey the commands from her brain.

He crouched beside her, slipping one arm across her back and one behind her thighs. She leaned into him and he lifted her from the floor and stood up in one motion.

He was careful to hold her body away from his as he carried her to the bed, but for her part she could've nestled in his arms forever. She wanted him to hold her and tell her this was all a joke.

He placed her on the bed with surprising gentleness. "Why don't you get some sleep, and we'll talk about this over breakfast?"

She grabbed a pillow and hugged it to her chest. "I wouldn't be able to sleep anyway. Tell me the truth. Tell me the whole ugly truth about what we were doing in that lab and why you stayed with Tempest."

He backed up and eased onto the edge of the bed across from hers. He blew out a long breath. "I stayed with Tempest even after I discovered their agenda because they wanted me to. Tempest controlled my mind and my body. They still do."

"No." Ava squeezed the pillow against her body, her fingers curling into soft foam.

"It's a form of brainwashing, Ava, but it goes beyond the brain. It's my body, too." He pushed up from the bed and plucked up a lamp with a metal rod from the base to the lightbulb. He unplugged it and removed the shade. Gripping it on either side with his hands, he bent it to a forty-five-degree angle. Then he held up the lamp by the lightbulb, which had to still be hot, and didn't even flinch.

Her eyes widened and her jaw dropped. "Dr. Arnoff's vitamin formula—stronger, faster, impervious to pain."

He released the bulb and the distorted lamp fell to the floor. He examined his hand. "So, he did tell you."

"That's what he was working on, but he told me it was years from completion."

He held up his reddened palm. "He completed it."

"What you're telling me—" she swung her legs over the side of the bed "—is crazy. You're saying that Dr. Arnoff's formula created some kind of superagent and that Tempest sent these agents out into the world to do its bidding?"

"Yes, but I told you it's more than physical." He tapped the side of his head. "Tempest messed with our minds, too."

She bunched the bedspread in her hands. "How? That didn't happen in our lab."

"No. That occurred in the debriefing unit in Germany where we went after every assignment."

She pinned her hands between her knees as

her eyes darted to the hotel door. Max Duvall could be crazy. This could all be some elaborate hallucination, one that he'd shared with Simon Skinner. Then her gaze tracked to the metal rod of the lamp, which he'd folded as if it were a straw. So, he was crazy *and* strong—a bad combination.

"How did they do it? The brainwashing?"

He squeezed his eyes closed and massaged his temple with two fingers. "Mind control—it was mind control and they did it through a combination of drugs, hypnosis and sleep therapy."

"What is sleep therapy?"

"That's my name for it. The doctors would hook us up to machines, brain scans, and then sedate us. They said it was for deep relaxation and stress reduction, but…" He shook his head.

"But what?" She wiped her palms on the bedspread. The air in the room almost crackled with electricity.

"It didn't do that. It didn't relax us, at least not me and Simon. After those sessions, a jumble of memories and scenes assaulted my brain. I couldn't tell real from fake. The memories— they implanted them in my brain."

She gasped as a bolt of fear shot through her chest. "They wanted you to forget the assignments."

"But I couldn't." He shoved off the window

and stalked across the room, pressing his palms against either side of his head. "Simon and I, we remembered. I don't know how many others did."

He really believed all of this, and he blamed her for administering the serum. Maybe the men at her house had been there to protect her from Max. The pressures of the job had driven them both off the deep end. Simon had snapped, and Max was nearing the same precipice.

"I-is that what drove Simon to commit violence? The implanted memories?"

"No." He pivoted and paced back to the window, a light sheen of sweat breaking out on his forehead. "The implanted memories were fine. It was the flashes of reality that tortured us."

If she kept pretending that she believed him, maybe he'd drop her off at the airport without incident. She could make up family somewhere, a family that cared about her and worried about her well-being. A fake family.

"The reality of what he'd done for Tempest pushed Simon past the breaking point?"

"It's the serum." He turned again and swayed to the side. He thrust out an unsteady hand to regain his balance. "Simon tried to break the cycle, but you can't go cold turkey. I told him not to go cold turkey."

A spasm of pain distorted his handsome

features, and Ava tensed her muscles to make a run at the door if necessary. "I'm not sure I understand, Max."

"The pills." He wiped a hand across his mouth and staggered. "I need the pills. I'll end up like Simon without them."

She braced her hands on her knees, ready to spring into action. The pills, again. He'd been going on about blue pills at the lab when he rescued her, too.

Max was talking gibberish now, his strong hands clenching and then unclenching, his gait unsteady, sweat dripping from his jaw.

"What pills?" She licked her lips. Her gaze flicked to the door. If she rolled off the other side of the bed, she could avoid Max, pitching and reeling in the middle of the room. Then she'd call 911. He needed help, but she didn't have the strength or the tools to subdue him if he decided to attack her.

"Pocket. The blue." Then he pitched forward and landed face-first on the floor.

Chapter Five

"Max!" She launched off the bed and crouched beside him. If he decided to grab her now, she wouldn't have a chance against his power.

His body twitched and he moaned. He *had* no power to grab her now. She could make a run for it and call hotel security. The hotel would call 911, and he could get help at the hospital from a doctor—a real doctor.

Max's dry lips parted, and he reached for her hand.

And if any part of his story was true? She knew the secrecy of that lab better than anyone. Those two men with the automatic weapons had been waiting at her house, for her. Max had saved her.

She curled her fingers around his and squeezed. "I'll be right back."

She ran to the bathroom and grabbed a hand towel. She held it under a stream of cool water and grabbed a bottle of the stuff on her way back to Max. She swept a pillow from the bed and sat on the floor beside his prone form.

He'd rolled to his back, so at least he wasn't unconscious.

Pressing two fingers against his neck, she checked his pulse—rapid but strong. She dabbed his face with the wet towel and eased a pillow beneath his head.

"Can you drink some water? Are you in any pain?" She held up the bottle.

"The pills." His voice rasped from his throat.

They were back to the pills? "What pills, Max?"

His hand dropped to his side, and she remembered what he'd said before he collapsed. His pocket.

She skimmed her hand across the rough material of one pocket and then the other, her fingers tracing the edges of a hard, square object. She dug her fingers into the pocket and pulled out a small tin of breath mints, but when she opened the lid no minty freshness greeted her.

Five round blue pills nestled together in the corner of the tin. She held up the container to his face. "These pills?"

His chin dipped to his chest, and she shook the pills into her palm.

He held up his index finger.

"Just one?"

He hissed, a sound that probably meant yes.

She picked up one pill between two fingers and placed it into his mouth. Then she held the water bottle up to his lips, while curling an arm around the back of his head to prop him up.

He swallowed the water and the pill disappeared. His spiky, dark lashes closed over his eyes and he melted against her arm. Her fingers burrowed into his thick, black hair as she dabbed his face with the towel.

His chest rose and fell, his breathing deeper and more regular. His face changed from a sickly pallor to his usual olive skin tone, and the trembling that had been racking his body ceased.

Whatever magic ingredient the little blue pill contained seemed to work. She peered at the remaining pills in the tin and sniffed them. Maybe he was a drug addict. Hallucinogens could bring on the paranoid thoughts.

His eyes flew open and he struggled to sit up.

"Whoa." Her arms slipped around his shoulders. "You just had a very scary incident. You need to lie back and relax."

"It passes quickly. I'm fine." He shrugged off her arm and sat up, leaning his back against the credenza. He chugged the rest of the water.

"Are you okay? I almost called 911."

"Don't—" he cinched her wrist with his thumb and middle finger "—ever call the police."

Her heart skipped a beat. She should've run when she had the chance.

His deep brown eyes widened and grew even darker. He dropped her wrist. "I'm sorry. I scared you."

She scooted away and rested her back against the bed, facing him. "And I'm sorry you're going through all this, but there's nothing I can do to help you. You need to see a doctor, and I—I'll go to my family and contact the CIA about what happened at the lab."

"You *are* a doctor." His eyes glittered through slits.

"Not exactly, and you know what I mean. You need to go to a doctor's office, get checked out."

"You mean a psychiatrist, don't you?"

"I mean…"

"You don't believe me. You're afraid of me. You think I'm crazy." He laughed, a harsh, stark sound with no humor in it.

"It's a crazy story, Max. My lab was just shot up and two men tried to kill me—or you."

"Both of us."

"Okay, maybe both of us, but I don't belong in the middle of all this."

"You're right." He rose from the floor, looking as strong and capable as ever. "Try to get some sleep. I'll take you to the airport tomorrow."

"And you?"

"I'll keep doing what I've been doing."

"Which is?"

"You don't belong in the middle of this, remember?" He tossed the pillow she'd tucked beneath him onto the bed and took a deep breath, the air in his lungs expanding his broad chest, his black T-shirt stretching across his muscles. "Would you like to take a shower? I need to take one, but you can go first."

"I would, but I can wait."

Still sitting on the floor, she'd stretched her legs in front of her.

Max stepped over her outstretched legs on the way to the bathroom and shut the door behind him.

Blowing out a long breath, Ava got to her feet and grabbed her purse. She could get a taxi to the airport before he even got out of the shower.

MAX BRACED HIS hands against the tile of the shower and dipped his head, as the warm water beat between his shoulder blades.

She'd be gone by the time he came out of the shower. And why shouldn't she be? She thought he was crazy. She didn't trust him. And she was right not to.

If she stayed, if she believed him, she could probably help him. She didn't seem to know about the pills, but she'd worked with Arnoff.

She might know something about those blue pills that stood between him and a complete melt-down like Simon.

He'd warned Simon to keep taking the pills, but his buddy was stubborn. He'd wanted nothing more to do with Tempest and its control over their lives.

Max faced the spray and sluiced the water through his hair. Maybe he'd made a mistake showing his hand to Tempest. As soon as he'd refused his last assignment, Foster had suspected he'd figured everything out—not everything. He and Simon hadn't realized quitting the serum would have such a profound effect on their bodies and minds.

He cranked off the water and grabbed a towel. At least he'd been able to save Dr. Whitman—Ava—from Simon. Stupid, stubborn bastard. Who was going to tell Simon's fiancée, Nina?

He dried off and wrapped the towel around his waist. A few hours' sleep would do him good, and then he'd reassess. He could contact Prospero, but he didn't know whom he could trust at this point. He didn't blame Ava one bit for high-tailing it out of here.

He pushed open the bathroom door and stopped short.

Ava looked up from examining something in the palm of her hand. Her gaze scanned his body, and he made a grab for the towel slipping down his hips.

"You're still here."

"Did you expect me to take off?"

He pointedly stared at the purse hanging over her shoulder. "Yeah."

She held out her hand, his precious pills cupped in her palm. "What are these? They have a distinctive odor."

"They should." He adjusted the towel again and glanced over his shoulder at his clothes scattered across the bathroom floor. He couldn't risk leaving her alone with those pills another minute. She might just get it in her head to run with them. She probably thought he was a junkie.

Her body stiffened and she closed her hand around the blue beauties. "Why would you say that?"

"They're a milder form of the serum you inject in us four times a year." He cocked his head. "You really don't know that?"

The color drained from her face, emphasizing her large eyes, which widened. "Why would you be taking additional doses of the serum?"

"Weaker doses. To keep up. To be better, faster, stronger, smarter. Isn't that what the serum is all about?"

"Did you know what they were when you started taking them?"

"By the time the pills were introduced into our regimen, we didn't care what they were for. We needed them."

"They're addictive?" She swept the breathmint tin from the credenza and funneled the pills into it from her cupped hand.

Max released the breath he'd been holding. "More than you could possibly know."

"Then tell me, Max. I deserve to know everything. I stayed." She shrugged the purse from her shoulder and tossed it onto the bed. "One little part of me believed your story. There was enough subterfuge in that lab to make me believe your wild accusations."

"Can I put my pants on first?" He hooked his fingers around the edge of the towel circling his hips.

Her eyes dropped to his hands, and the color came rushing back into her pale cheeks. "Of course. I'm not going anywhere."

He retreated to the bathroom and dropped the towel. Leaning close to the mirror, he plowed a hand through his damp hair. It needed a trim and he needed a shave, not that he'd given a damn about his appearance before Ava came onto the scene.

He pulled on his camos and returned to the bedroom.

Ava had moved to the chair and sat with her

legs curled beneath her, a look of expectancy highlighting her face.

He'd memorized that face from his quarterly visits with her. Dr. Ava Whitman had been the one bright spot in the dark tunnel of Tempest. He believed with certainty that she had no idea what she'd been dosing them with. At first, he'd been incredulous that a doctor wouldn't know what was in a formula she was giving her patients, but her story made sense. Tempest sought out the most vulnerable. The agency used blackmail and coercion, and in Ava's case, hope, to recruit people.

Dr. Arnoff had kept her in the dark, had probably shut down her questions by reminding her that she wouldn't be working as a doctor if it weren't for the agency and then using the illegality of that work to keep her in line.

And she'd been good at her job. He had a hard time remembering the two missions he'd been on last year, but he could clearly recall Ava's soft touch and cheery tone as she checked his vitals and injected him with the serum that would destroy his life.

Ava cleared her throat. "If the blue pills are a weaker dose of the T-101 serum, why are you still taking them?"

"I have to."

"Because you're addicted? Why not just ride

out the withdrawal?" She laced her fingers in her lap. "I can help you. I—I have some experience with that."

He raised his eyebrows. She had to be referring to a patient. "It's more than the addiction. I could ride that out. You saw Simon."

She drew in a quick breath and hunched forward. "Simon went over the edge. He lost it. The stress, the tension, maybe even the brainwashing—they all did him in."

"It's the...T-101, Ava. Is that what you called it? Without the serum, we self-destruct. Another agent, before Simon, before me, he committed suicide. Tempest put it down to post-traumatic stress disorder because this agent had killed a child by mistake on a raid. Now I wonder if that was even a mistake or his true assignment."

"Adam Belchik." She drew her knees to her chest, wrapping her arms around them.

"That's right. I thought he was before your time."

"He was, but I heard about him."

"He was the first to go off the meds, and he paid the price. He had a family, so he killed himself before he could harm them."

"Is that why you were jabbering about cold turkey? You can't quit cold turkey like Simon did, like Adam did. You have to keep lowering your dosage by continuing with the blue pills."

"That's it." He pointed to the tin on the credenza, the fine line keeping him from insanity and rage. "I find if I take one a day, I can maintain. I tried a half, and it didn't work."

"You have only five left." Her gaze darted to the credenza and back to his face.

"Four now. Four pills. Four days."

She uncurled her legs and almost fell out of the chair as she bolted from it. "That's crazy. What happens at the end of the four days?"

He lifted his shoulders. "I'll be subject to incidents like the one you just witnessed until they kill me or I snap...or Tempest gets to me first."

"And if they do?"

"They'll either kill me or I'll be their drone for the rest of my life."

She folded her arms across her stomach, clutching the material of her blouse at her sides. "There has to be another way. If we get more of the pills and you take smaller and smaller doses, maybe eventually you can break free. You tried taking a half, but it was too soon."

"Where would I get more pills? You said yourself you never saw them at the lab. They weren't administered at the lab. My quick search there revealed nothing."

She snapped her fingers. "Max, there has to be an antidote somewhere."

"Why would you think that? Tempest had no intention of ever reversing the damage they'd done to us."

"Maybe not to you, but Dr. Arnoff tested the T-101 on himself."

His heart slammed against his chest. "Are you sure?"

"I'm positive, or at least I'm positive that he told me he'd tried it on himself. He said he felt like a superhero—strong, invincible, sexually potent."

She reddened to the edge of her hairline and waved a hand in the air. "You know, that's what he said."

Sexual potency? It had been a long time since he'd been close enough to a woman in a normal situation to even think about sex.

He cleared his throat. "If he acted as his own guinea pig, he'd want something to counteract the effects in case things didn't go the way he planned."

"Exactly—an antidote."

"We could be jumping to conclusions." He dragged in a breath and let it out slowly in an attempt to temper his excitement. He'd learned to be cautious about good news. "Maybe Arnoff didn't develop an antidote. He could've dialed back by taking the blue pills—fewer and fewer of them until the cravings stopped and the physical effects dissipated."

"That could be, but it also means there must be more of those blue pills floating around." She dropped onto the bed. "What about the other agents? Can you all pool your resources and wean yourselves off of the serum?"

He cracked a smile and shook his head.

"What's so funny? That's the first real smile I've seen from you all night, and I wasn't even making a joke."

"I just got a visual of a bunch of Tempest agents sitting around a campfire sharing little pieces of their blue pills."

A smile hovered at her lips. "Not possible?"

"I don't even know who more than half of the agents are."

"I do."

His gaze locked onto hers. "You don't know all their names. You don't know where they live, and most of them are probably on assignment anyway."

She shook her finger at him. "You'd be surprised how many of them opened up to me."

"Not surprised at all." She'd obviously been a ray of sunshine for the other agents, too. "But we can't go knocking on their doors asking them to give up their meds. Unless they've already suspected something or had incidents like Simon and I did, they're not going to see the problem."

"I meant to ask you that." She fell back against the mattress and rolled to her side to face him, propping up her head with one hand. "What made you and Simon realize what was going on?"

"There were gaps, glitches in our response to the treatment. For me it was the memories. I recalled too much about my operations. The memories they tried to implant in my brain didn't jibe with my reality. On one assignment, Simon and I started comparing notes and then experimenting with the pills."

"Simon didn't show up for his last appointment with me. He never got his injection."

"He decided to make a clean break. He shrugged off the seizures even though I tried to warn him." He dropped his head in his hands, digging his fingers into his scalp. What would they tell Simon's fiancée?

The bed sank beside him, and he turned his head as Ava touched his back.

"You had to shoot Simon. He would've killed you. He would've killed me." The pressure of her hand between his shoulder blades increased. "Now, since you saved my life—twice—I'm going to save yours."

He wanted to believe her. He wanted to stretch out on the bed next to Ava and feel her soft touch on his forehead again.

"And how to you propose to do that, Dr. Whitman?"

Her hand dropped from his back. "Don't call me that. I told you, I never finished. I don't deserve the title."

"Ava."

"We're going to find that antidote or a million blue pills to get you through this." She yawned and covered her mouth with the back of her hand. "But first I'm going to sleep away the rest of what's left of this evening."

"And your family? I thought I was taking you to the airport tomorrow so you could fly out to be with your family."

"My family." She launched from his bed to hers, peeled back the covers and slipped beneath them. "I have no family."

Chapter Six

Ava buried her head beneath a pillow and ran her tongue along her teeth. She needed a toothbrush and a meal.

"Are you awake?"

Lifting one corner of the pillow, she peered out at Max sitting in front of a tablet computer at the table by the window. "What time is it?"

He flicked back the heavy drapes and a spear of sunlight sliced through the room. "It's around ten o'clock. You must be hungry. When was the last time you ate?"

"I had my dinner at the lab before…before everything went down."

"That was a long time ago."

"An eternity. A lifetime." She retreated beneath the pillow. How was she supposed to do this with Max? Why did her life always manage to get upended?

She heard his footsteps across the room and the crackle of plastic.

"I went down to the little store in the hotel and bought you a few things."

"A new life?"

The silence yawned from across the room and engulfed her. She tossed the pillow away from her and sat up.

Max stood in the center of the room, a plastic bag dangling at his side. "You don't need to do this, Ava. In fact, I'm going to take you to the airport right now. I'll pay for a ticket anywhere you want to go. Then you can call the CIA or whatever number the lab gave you in case of an emergency and you can forget about all of this."

She sighed. "I was trying to make a joke. I want to help you. I feel responsible for your predicament. If I hadn't been so anxious for a job, any job, I wouldn't have been injecting you and Simon and countless others with poison."

"Not your fault. They would've found someone else." He chucked the bag onto the foot of the bed. "Toothbrush, comb, deodorant, some other stuff. Take a shower. I have some stuff to get out of the car, and then I'll meet you in the restaurant downstairs for breakfast. You can let me know then what you want to do."

The door closed behind him and she stared at it for several seconds. A ticket to anywhere. A new start—again. How many new starts did one woman need?

She threw off the covers and grabbed the bag of toiletries. She didn't need a new start. She needed a finish. She needed to help Max Duvall.

Forty minutes later, freshly showered but wearing the same clothes from yesterday, Ava made her way down to the lobby. She spotted Max immediately. Did everyone else notice the aura of power and menace around him or did she just have that special switch that flicked on when danger sent out its Siren's call?

He glanced up from his newspaper and watched her approach with an unwavering gaze, as if willing her to his side. He didn't have to throw out any lures. She was all in.

He rose to his feet when she reached the table and pulled out her chair. "Do you feel better after your shower?"

Sitting down, she flicked the collar of her blouse. "I'd feel even better if I had some clean clothes to step into."

"I wouldn't recommend going back to your house for a while."

"Ever?" She turned her coffee cup over and nodded at the waitress bearing a coffeepot.

"When this all blows over."

"When will that be?" After the waitress came by with the coffee, Ava poured a steady stream of cream into her cup, watching the milky swirls fan out in the dark liquid.

"When the CIA or Prospero gets a handle on Tempest and puts a stop to its clandestine operations."

The spoon hovered over her cup. "In other words, I'd better get used to these clothes."

"Buy new ones."

"Is that what you do?" She took in the dark blue T-shirt, very similar to the black T-shirt he'd been wearing last night. He'd swapped the camouflage pants for a pair of faded jeans.

"I've been carrying my clothes—and everything else—with me for the past month. I have one bag for my clothes and a second one for my...tools."

She slurped a sip of coffee, wondering how best to ask him about his tools, when the waitress came back and saved her from doing something stupid.

They both asked for omelets, but Max added a bowl of oatmeal and some fresh fruit to his order.

She folded her hands on the table and tilted her head. "When was the last time you ate?"

"It's been a while." He brought the coffee cup to his lips and stared at her over the rim. "Airport?"

She gripped her hands together and sucked in a breath. She let it out on one word. "No."

"Are you sure?"

"I have some ideas, Max."

The waitress placed Max's oatmeal between them, and he dumped some brown sugar and raisins into the bowl. "I'm listening."

The maple smell of the brown sugar rose on the steam, creating a homey feel completely at odds with their conversation.

"I know where Dr. Arnoff lives—lived." She pushed her cup out of the way and tapped a spot on the table. "The lab is here and Albuquerque is this way. He lives in a suburb, a high-end suburb. We can start with his house and see if he has anything there, any of those blue pills. I know he keeps a work laptop at home."

"Is he married? Does he have a family?"

"He is married, but his children are adults. One lives overseas and the other one is in Boston."

"You think his wife, his widow, is going to invite us into her home so we can snoop around in her dead husband's personal effects?" He plunged his spoon into the oatmeal.

"You're a spy, aren't you? We either break in or gain entrance through some kind of subterfuge."

He raised an eyebrow. "I repeat. You do not have to do any of this. You can hop on a plane and put this behind you."

"No, I can't." Whatever happened, she'd never forget Max Duvall. She'd always wonder if he made it or not, and if he didn't make it she'd always blame herself.

He left his spoon in the bowl and pushed it to the corner of the table. "You mentioned you had no family. Do you have friends you can stay with?"

"Out of the blue like this?" She spread her hands. "No."

"If anything happened to you…"

She pressed her fingers against his forearm, and his corded muscle twitched beneath her touch. "I'll be with you. For better or worse, you still have T-101 pulsing through your system. You're practically indestructible."

"I may be, but you're not." He covered her hand with his own, his touch rough, awkward but sincere. "You can give me directions to Arnoff's and I'll go there on my own."

"What am I supposed to do? Where am I supposed to go?"

They broke apart when the waitress delivered their food. "You had the Denver and you had the spinach? Ketchup? Salsa?"

"Both, please." Ava flicked the napkin into her lap.

When the waitress returned with their condiments, Max spooned some salsa onto his plate and took up the conversation without missing a beat. "You can stay here."

"Stay here?"

"I'd come back after going to Arnoff's in case nothing panned out there. You could help me find a few other agents and be on your way." He sawed off an edge of his omelet with his fork. "Once you decide where you want to go."

"I'd need to call the CIA or rather the emergency number I have."

"You have an emergency number?"

"I thought I told you that." She stabbed a potato and dragged it through the puddle of ketchup on her plate. Then she remembered the blood all over the lab and placed the tines of her fork on the edge of her plate.

"You told me you planned to call the CIA."

"Yeah, the emergency number."

"You know for a fact that the emergency number goes to the CIA?"

"I just assumed it did." She wrapped her hands around her cup, still warm from the coffee the waitress had topped off. "D-do you think it's the number for someone at Tempest?"

"Could be." The blood-red ketchup didn't seem to bother him as he squirted another circle of it on the side of his plate.

Her hands tightened around the mug. "I can't call that number. Those men at my house could've been from Tempest."

"They *were* from Tempest." He tapped her plate with his knife. "Eat your breakfast."

She spooned the ketchup from her plate into a napkin. "So, who am I supposed to call? The number for the CIA isn't exactly in the phone book."

"You should call Prospero—once I'm out of the picture."

"You don't trust Prospero but you expect me to?"

"You're not an agent formerly working with Tempest. Prospero has no reason not to trust you."

"Really? Because you trusted me immediately?"

"I can't trust anyone, Ava."

"Maybe I can't either."

"You can trust me."

"As long as you keep taking the reduced dosage of T-101 in those pills."

He glanced up from his plate, his dark eyes narrowing to slits. "I'm glad you recognize that. Don't forget it."

His tone made her a little breathless. What would she do if Max turned into Simon? She'd have to be long gone before that ever happened. He'd make himself long gone before that ever happened.

She finished her omelet and put her hand over her cup when the waitress swung by to offer refills.

Max pushed his plate away and crumpled up a napkin next to it. "Do you have Arnoff's address?"

"Yes. When are you going out there?"

"I think it's best if I wait until night."

"In case Mrs. Arnoff isn't cooperative?"

His hand jerked and the water in the glass he'd been holding sloshed and the ice tinkled. "I wouldn't hurt Dr. Arnoff's wife."

Her cheeks burned. "I didn't mean that at all. I just... I mean in case you have to break in or something."

His shallow breath deepened and he seemed to unclench his jaw. "I won't hurt her. I won't do that."

She didn't want to probe too deeply into whether or not he'd hurt civilians for Tempest. Whatever he'd done for the agency, it disturbed him profoundly.

"She must know by now her husband's dead. Maybe she's not even home." She patted the newspaper on the chair between them. "I suppose there's nothing in the paper about the mayhem at the lab."

"No journalists even know about the lab, do they? Do the police in that area make a habit of patrolling around the lab?"

"No. We had our own security force. No police."

"They knew it was there?"

"They knew it was a top secret government entity. The lab's security force had given the local cops instructions to keep their distance."

"Then maybe nothing's been discovered yet. Did family members ever drop by?"

"I..."

"Other employees' family members."

She pursed her lips. She hadn't been about to tell him she had no family again. Guess she'd already beaten that particular dead horse. "I was going to say, I never saw any family members there. A lot of the lab employees didn't even reside in New Mexico. They lived elsewhere and had come out here for the assignment. I got the impression most left their families behind."

"Except Dr. Arnoff."

"He was the head of the lab, so he was a permanent fixture."

"Did he tend to work long hours? Sleep at the lab?"

"He did."

"Then his wife may not even know he's dead."

"Perhaps not. You're not going to tell her, are you?"

He held up his hands. "Not me, and I doubt if she'd take kindly to a stranger snooping around and asking questions."

She sat forward in her chair, hunching over the table. "That's why I need to go with you. I'm sure she remembers me. We met a few times. I can get us into the house by telling her Dr. Arnoff sent me to collect something. Once we're in the house, you can do your spy thing."

"As you delicately pointed out before, I can get into the house and she'll never know I was there."

"But my way might be easier."

"I think you'd be safer here at the hotel."

Folding her arms, she sat back in her chair while Max left some money on the check tray. He didn't plan to leave until dark, so she still had some time to work on him. "What are your plans in the meantime?"

"Shopping."

"A little retail therapy? I never would've guessed you were the sort."

He waved his finger up and down to take in her wrinkled blouse. "I was thinking of you. Do you want to pick up a few clothes here?"

"That would be great, but you don't have to come along."

"Humor me."

FOR THE NEXT few hours, she humored him. She picked up some jeans and T-shirts, a comfortable pair of ankle boots and some sneakers. She added some underwear and a few more toiletries. Max picked out a small carry-on suitcase for the plane trip he was convinced she'd be taking. She let him believe that.

He paid cash for everything from a seemingly endless supply of money even when she offered to use her credit card, which he refused and told her to put away.

She wasn't going to allow him to pay for everything, so when he ducked into a sandwich shop to get some drinks she headed toward an ATM.

Placing the edge of her card at the slot, her hand wavered. It had to be okay to use her card just once. The machine piled up the bills for her to snatch. She tucked them into her purse and returned to the front of the sandwich shop.

Max approached her, carrying two drinks in front of him. "Are you going to get that other pair of shoes?"

"No, I decided against it. I don't want to spend

any more of your money." She held out her own cash to him. "And I really want to pay you back."

Max reached out and squeezed her shoulder. "Don't worry about it. I appreciate the gesture, but you keep the cash just in case." He handed her a soda and picked up her shopping bags. "I don't know about you, but I need a nap after last night's activities."

She could use a nap, too, but sleeping in the same room as Max was awkward—at least for her. He seemed all business now, definitely not as friendly as when he was her patient. But he hadn't known the extent of his enslavement to Tempest at that point and that she'd been injecting him with poison. He had no reason to be friendly to her.

He'd parked his car in the parking structure below the mall, and they took the elevator into the bowels of the garage.

As they approached the blue sedan, she turned to him suddenly. "Where'd you get this car? Why do you have all that cash?"

He clicked the remote and put a finger to his lips. "I still have some secrets."

She eyed the car as he opened the trunk and swung her bags inside. It didn't look like a spy's car unless it had special, hidden gadgets.

"Does this thing have an ejection seat or turn into a hovercraft?"

He opened the passenger door for her and cocked his head. "I don't think it can even do eighty miles an hour."

The car went sixty on the highway on the way back to the hotel. Max rolled into the hotel's parking garage, and they returned to the room.

He pulled the drapes closed on the gray day and stretched out on the bed with his tablet propped up on his knees.

She pointed at the computer. "I thought you were going to sleep."

"I am. I'm actually reading a book. Even though it's a good one, I should be drifting off any minute—and you should, too."

She sat on the edge of the bed and toed off her shoes. Then she fell backward, her knees bent and her feet still planted on the floor, and stared at the ceiling.

She should've never taken the job offer from Dr. Arnoff. It had seemed too good to be true— a chance to practice medicine without the medical license. Now she was paying for her lies. She always did.

"Do you generally sleep with your legs hanging off the bed?"

"I'm almost too tired to move."

"Shopping does that to me, too."

"I don't think it was the shopping." She hoisted herself up on her elbows. "I think it's more the threats on my life and the fact that my job was a sham."

"Sorry."

She studied his face. Was he being sarcastic?

He stared back at her, his dark eyes serious, not a hint of sarcasm. Had he lost that ability, too?

No, he meant it. His life was in the toilet and he still had empathy for her. Guess the T-101 hadn't worked that great on him if it had been designed to erase human emotions. Max kept a tight rein on his feelings, but he definitely had them.

"Thanks. I'm sorry, too. Sorry that you're going through this. Sorry that I was a party to it."

He dropped his gaze to his book. "Let's try to get some sleep."

Folding her legs on the bed, she rolled to her side and closed her eyes. If Max thought he was leaving her here when he went to Dr. Arnoff's, he had another think coming.

This agent, this damaged man, was her only hope of returning to a life with any semblance of normalcy—not that she'd ever had that before.

THIS TIME SHE woke up first. She scooted to the edge of the mattress and peered through the gloom at Max fast asleep on the other bed, the tablet rising and falling on his chest with every deep breath.

Even in repose, sleeping on his back, he looked primed and ready. Could he ever really relax?

She rolled to the other side of the bed and slipped off the edge. Tiptoeing around the room, she gathered a few of her new purchases and retreated to the bathroom.

She peeled off the clothes she'd dressed in yesterday morning, never dreaming she was heading into a nightmare, one worse than the previous nightmare she'd already lived through.

Did the nightmares ever end?

She brushed her teeth and washed her face. She dabbed on some moisturizer and added a little makeup. She didn't want to scare Mrs. Arnoff before she could talk her way into the house.

She padded on bare feet back into the room, her dirty clothes tucked under one arm, her shoes hanging from her fingertips.

"I was getting used to those slacks and blouse."

She jumped and dropped a shoe.

In the darkness of the room, Max was watching her from the bed, a pillow wedged beneath his neck.

She swept the shoe from the floor and stacked the armful of clothes on top of the suitcase Max had bought, still believing she would hop on a plane to somewhere.

"If I never see these slacks again, it will be too soon. I could toss them down the trash chute and be perfectly happy." She scraped at a spot on the navy blue pant leg. "Th-there are spots of blood on them that I never noticed before."

"You can send them to the dry cleaner while you wait for me." He swung his legs from the bed, raising his arms above his head in a long stretch.

"Yeah, about that." She busied her hands folding the clothes. "I'm going with you."

"No." He dropped his arms and shoved off the bed. "I have no idea what I'm going to find at Arnoff's house."

"You're probably going to find Mrs. Arnoff." She wedged her hands on her hips. "She knows me. She'll let me in the house. She'll let me go through her husband's things if I tell her he sent me. She'll give me his computer."

"Unless she knows he's dead somehow."

"I don't think she will. You said yourself that news of the lab won't leak out until everything's cleaned up. And if she does—" she shrugged "—I'll make up another story to get us inside based on what she thinks she knows."

"Why are you so hell-bent on coming along? You don't owe me anything. I believe you that you knew nothing about the T-101 and Tempest's true mission."

"I'm not volunteering out of a sense of guilt." Clearly, she needed to use a new justification. "I don't want you to leave me here alone. You're the only person who can help me now, the only one I can turn to."

His nostrils flared. "Are you really afraid to stay here by yourself?"

"I'd feel better if I came along with you." She waved a hand at the window. "I don't know what's out there. I don't know who's out there, and I'm certainly not prepared to meet them if they come after me."

He crossed to the window and pressed his forehead against the glass as if assessing the danger below. "I think you'd be fine here, but if you're not comfortable, you can come with me."

Ava released a measured breath, not quite a sigh. "I would feel more comfortable, and I think I can get us into the house."

He held up his hand. "We'll see when we get there. I'm going to brush my teeth and get some gear together."

It was exactly that gear she was counting on to keep her safe. She'd played on Max's natural protective instincts to get him to agree to let her come along, but it hadn't been a total ruse. What would she do here alone? What would she do if someone came after her?

For now she'd stick to Max and his gear.

While he got ready, she turned on the TV, not that she expected to see any news about the lab. Tempest or the CIA would clamp down on that story. When she and Max parted ways, could she trust the CIA? Tempest had presumably been operating, unchecked, right under the nose of the agency.

Max slung a bag across his chest, gripping the strap with one hand. "Are you ready?"

She'd think about whom to trust when she and Max parted once they reached that point. She hadn't been lying to him. Right now, he was all she had.

She tossed the remote control on the bed. "Ready."

They took the elevator to the second floor and then jogged down the stairwell, their shoes slapping against the metal steps.

Max pushed through the fire door and she followed him across a short hallway to a side exit that led to the parking structure.

The parking lot had cleared out some since they'd returned to the hotel from shopping, and it looked as if they'd missed the dinner crowd leaving for their restaurants.

Max unlocked the car and hoisted his bag into the backseat.

She scrambled into the passenger side of the car before he could change his mind.

They snapped their seat belts in unison and Max slipped the key into the ignition. It clicked.

"What the…?" His fingers hovered over the dangling keys.

Ava's nostrils flared. "What's that smell?"

"Ava, get out!" He yanked off his seat belt as she stared at him with her mouth agape.

He popped the release for her and then nudged her shoulder. "Get out of the car now and run for the exit!"

He reached into the backseat and a surge of adrenaline pulsed through her veins. She snagged her bag from the floor of the car and shoved at the door. It fell open and she stumbled out of the car.

"Get to the stairwell." Max sprinted behind the car, the black bag banging against his hip.

She didn't know why the hell they were running, but when Max Duvall yelled "run" in that tone of voice, she obeyed.

He crowded behind her, urging her to move faster.

Just when she smacked her palms against the cold metal of the stairwell door, an explosion rocked her off her feet, driving her against the door.

As Max smashed against her back, she jerked her head over her shoulder—just in time to see their ride go up in flames.

Chapter Seven

Max cranked his head around, squinting through the black, acrid smoke billowing from his stolen car. No collateral damage. *Please, God, no civilians.*

He peeled himself away from Ava, flattened against the stairwell door. "Are you okay?"

She nodded, covering her ears with her hands.

The noise from the explosion hadn't affected him. He still had enough T-101 coursing through his bloodstream to make him immune to such things.

"Did you see anyone else up here when we went to the car?"

"What?"

He put his lips close to her ear, which had to be ringing. "Any other people. Was anyone else on this level?"

"I didn't see anyone."

"Let's get out of here." He reached around her and pressed the door handle down. The door swung open, and he had to catch Ava around the waist as she tripped.

They'd been discovered. How?

Footsteps echoed in the stairwell, and Max pulled the gun from its shoulder holster and held it against his chest, beneath his jacket.

A man and two women, faces white, eyes wide, met them on the next landing. The man gripped the handrail. "What happened?"

"A car on level four is on fire."

"Fire?" One of the women grabbed the man's arm. "That sounded like an explosion."

Max shrugged. "I don't know. Maybe the flames reached the gas tank. We called 911."

As if on cue sirens called in the distance.

Ava put her hand out. "I wouldn't go up there. It's dangerous. Let the firemen handle it."

The man asked, "Nobody's up there? Nobody in the car?"

"No." Max grabbed Ava's hand and tugged her downstairs. He whispered in her ear. "When we get to the hotel room, throw your things in that suitcase. We're out of here."

Back in the room, Ava moved like a robot, but at least she moved like a fast robot. She swept the items she'd bought that afternoon into the new bag without one question on her lips. Despite the quick movements, she had a dazed expression on her face. That would change to fear soon enough when the shock wore off.

By the time they returned to the garage, the fire department had cordoned off every level except the first. In the confusion, people had abandoned their cars in the circular driveway. Max scanned the cars lined up, waiting for the valet.

"This one." He propelled Ava toward an older SUV with its hatchback open. He threw his bags in the back and pried her suitcase from her fingers and tossed it in after his.

With his hand against the small of her back he maneuvered her to the passenger side of the car. She stalled and for a minute he thought he was going to have to pick her up and drop her on the seat.

Then she placed one foot on the running board and he helped her inside.

Glancing around him at the chaos, he strode to the other side of the car, turned the keys dangling from the ignition and rolled away from the curb.

He paused to let another fire engine careen into the garage, and then he floored the accelerator and whipped around the corner.

Ava kept her eyes glued to the street in front of them as he dodged between cars, glancing at his rearview and side mirrors at every turn.

Tempest had tracked them down. He'd figured someone had been monitoring the cameras at the lab, and chances were his car had been made. He should've ditched it at the first possible opportunity instead of shopping with Ava.

He'd let his guard down.

As he zigzagged around the city making sure to lose any possible tail, Ava maintained a stony silence on her side of the car. His eyes darted to the side once or twice to make sure she was still breathing.

At the end of his circuitous route, he took one more look at his mirrors and headed for the freeway on-ramp. They still had a date with Dr. Arnoff's widow.

Ten minutes later, Ava shifted in her seat and expelled a long breath.

"Are you okay?"

"It's my fault."

He swiped a hand in the air between them. "Don't be ridiculous. It was my idea to go shopping. We probably should've just stayed in the room and left the car in the parking lot."

"No." She hiccuped and then covered her mouth with her fingers. "I led them to us by using my ATM card."

His gut rolled. "You used your ATM card?"

She nodded, covering her face with her hands. "I'm sorry. I didn't think. I didn't realize."

"When? At the mall when I was getting

drinks?" He opened and closed his hands on the steering wheel. He shouldn't have left her alone for a second.

"Yes. I—I just wanted to pay you back. I guess it never occurred to me that they could track me that way." She dragged her fingers through her long, chestnut-brown hair and sighed. "That's not true. I had a moment right when I stuck the card in the slot, a moment of panic."

"Why didn't you tell me?"

"I convinced myself it meant nothing. It was too scary to contemplate that someone would be tracking me."

A muscle ticked in his jaw. He couldn't expect Ava to have the same instincts that he did. He should've warned her against using her cards. Obviously, she didn't understand the significance of the large amounts of cash he carried with him. Or she understood the importance for him but not herself. It probably was a form of denial.

Hunching his shoulders, he braced his hands against the steering wheel and extended his arms. "Don't worry about it now. It's a done deal."

"Your car…"

"Not mine."

"Stolen like this one?"

"Yes."

She blew out a ragged breath. "How did they find the car? How did they know what you were driving?"

"They probably have it on video from the cameras at the lab. I tried to take out as many cameras as I saw on my way into the lab, but I'm sure there were others hidden from view. Once you used your card at the mall, they knew where to look. They could've trained a satellite on the area."

"They're relentless, aren't they?"

"That's one word for it."

"And they have the advantage because they know who we are, and they're just some nameless, faceless assassins to us."

"Maybe, maybe not." He slowed the stolen SUV until the car behind them passed on the left and sped out of sight.

"Do you think you might know the man or men after us?"

"I might and you might if Tempest is sending its agents to take care of us."

She pinned her hands between her bouncing knees. "I can't imagine even one of my patients trying to kill me."

"Have you forgotten Simon already? Your patients, as you call them, are programmed to do just that. Tempest will tell lies to get them to do the job. Keep your eyes open for a familiar face."

"Ugh." She wrapped her arms around herself. "Where are we going now?"

"Dr. Arnoff's house, as planned."

She whipped her head around to face him. "Won't Tempest figure we'll be heading there?"

He squinted into the rearview mirror at a pair of headlights behind them and then let out a breath when the car turned off. "Tempest doesn't know what I know. They don't know if I've gone off the rails like Simon or if I've put any of the puzzle pieces together yet. That car bomb was meant to kill me or warn me."

"Uh, it blew up that car. I think the message was pretty clear."

He held up a finger. "Ah, but it didn't ignite right away. It's not like Tempest to make a mistake like that. As soon as I turned on the ignition, I sensed the danger. They had to know I'd figure it out."

"And if you hadn't?"

He shrugged. "We'd both be dead."

Her body stiffened and he silently cursed his insensitivity. She wasn't like him—cold, unfeeling.

"Sorry." His hand shot out and covered hers, clutching her thigh. His fingertips brushed her soft skin, and he felt her tremble. He slid his hand from hers and rested it on the console between them.

"Anyway, Tempest might not realize I need to search Arnoff's house. They know I know he's dead—end of story."

"And if they *are* at his house?"

"We'll take every precaution. Going to Arnoff's is worth the risk."

"If you say so. They'd probably figure us for a couple of lunatics going to Arnoff's after that car bomb, so we just might be safe."

"I can drop you off on the way, Ava." He wiped one palm on his jeans. "I can still take you to the airport."

"Then what? I go underground? Go into the witness protection program for spies?"

"I told you. Prospero can help you. You get on a plane to anywhere and call Prospero once you reach your destination. I can give you a contact number."

"You implied earlier that you couldn't trust Prospero."

"I can't trust anyone, but once you separate from me, you should be okay. You can tell them whatever you want. Just don't tell them you believed me. Tell them I'm insane. Tell them I held you against your will."

"What about you?"

"I'll figure it out."

"You'll figure it out a lot faster with me by your side. I may not be a real doctor, but I'm familiar with formulas, especially this one. If there's an antidote out there, I'm going to recognize it faster than you will."

"I appreciate the offer, but…"

She pounded the dashboard. "You keep getting this crazy idea that I'm doing this for your benefit. Don't you get it? I don't have anywhere else to go. You're it. You're my protector whether you want to be or not."

He wanted to be. The thought came out of nowhere and slammed against his chest. Just as quickly, he stuffed it away.

Skimming his palms along the steering wheel, he said, "It's going to be dangerous. I can't guarantee your safety."

"You've done a pretty good job of it so far." She jabbed a finger at the windshield. "Two more exits."

"Do me a favor when we get there."

She crossed her arms and gave him a wary look. "What?"

"Follow my lead."

"I've been doing that ever since you dragged me out of the lab."

"Any complaints?"

"I'm alive, aren't I?"

So far they both were and he intended to keep it that way.

Following her directions, he maneuvered the

car through a well-heeled neighborhood. Looked like being employed as a mad scientist had its rewards.

Ava pulled a slip of paper from the pocket of her hoodie and peered at it. "Have we hit Hopi Drive yet?"

"Nope."

"It should be coming up."

"I'm not driving up and parking in front of the house. I'll drive by first and tuck the car away somewhere."

"Good idea, considering it's stolen."

"Any complaints?"

"Considering our car had been…disabled, none at all."

She directed him to Dr. Arnoff's house, and he slowed the car down to a crawl as he passed in front of it. Lights burned somewhere in the house and a late-model Mercedes crouched in the driveway.

"Do you know if that's Arnoff's car?"

"It's his wife's. He drives a Caddy and as far as I know it's still at the lab."

He wheeled around the corner, made a U-turn and parked at the curb. "I'm going to leave the doors unlocked and the key in the ignition. If anything happens in there, make a run for it. Take the car and don't look back."

Her tongue darted from her mouth and swept across her lower lip. "I'd wait for you."

"That might not be an option."

He cracked the door and she put a hand on his arm. "Are you really expecting trouble?"

"I always expect trouble."

She slid from the car and dropped to the ground on silent sneakers and then pushed the door closed. *Good.* He didn't have to tell her to be quiet. She was a fast learner.

"I hope nobody steals the car."

A dog barked in the distance and another howled an answer. Max put a finger to his lips.

He held out his hand behind him and she took it. Then he hunched over and crossed the street, pulling Ava close in his wake. Might as well not make it easy for someone watching to distinguish two figures in the night, even though they planned to knock on the front door.

When they reached the other side of the street, Max followed the hedges bordering the sidewalk, the shoulder of his jacket brushing the stiff leaves.

He tucked Ava behind him as he edged around the corner, glancing up and down the block. Lights dotted the houses along the quiet residential neighborhood, but everyone must've turned in early for the night.

He kept to the available shadows and Ava

stuck close to him, the flowery perfume she'd gotten at the department store tickling his nostrils.

They made their way up the driveway, skirting the luxury car. The porch light created a yellow crescent, encompassing the porch and a flower bed under the window. The fragrance from the colorful blooms matched the scent wafting from Ava.

Funny how smells could distinguish a place and time. Whatever happened, the particular smell of those flowers would always remind him of this night with Ava. No drug could take that away from him.

She whispered, "Are we going to knock? Unless she's already heard about the lab, she won't be surprised to see me."

"Go ahead."

Max turned and faced the street as she rang the doorbell. A footfall from inside the house had Ava standing up straight and plastering a smile on her face.

A muffled voice reached them through the heavy door. "Who is it?"

"Mrs. Arnoff, it's Ava Whitman—from the lab?"

A chain scraped and the door eased open. Mrs. Arnoff, a robe wrapped around her body, peered at them. "I thought that was you. Is everything okay at the lab?"

Mrs. Arnoff didn't know.

Ava widened her smile until her cheeks hurt. "Everything's fine. Dr. Arnoff is hard at work and sent me over to pick up a few things for him."

The door swung open. "I've been trying to call him for two days. He didn't mention that he was spending the night at the lab this time."

"You know how it gets there sometimes— crazy and our cell phone reception is nonexistent."

"He usually does get out to call me though." Her gaze shifted to Max. "Come on in."

Ava waved her hand at Max. "This is…Mike, my friend."

"Hello, Mike." Mrs. Arnoff offered her hand to Max. "I'm glad to see Ava has made some friends."

Ava winced. So, Dr. Arnoff had told his wife about her pathetic social existence.

"Ava and I have been friends for a while." Max draped his arm across her shoulder.

For a man with no emotions, he sure seemed to be getting into this role.

Mrs. Arnoff gestured to a half-full wineglass on the coffee table in front of the muted TV. "Would you like some wine? Something else?"

Ava folded her hands in front of her, trying not to twist her fingers. "No, thank you, Mrs. Arnoff."

"Lillian—please call me Lillian. I feel like I know you even though we've met just a few times. Charles talks about you a lot."

"Really?" Ava coughed. "Dr. Arnoff is brilliant. I'm so lucky to be working with him."

"Well, the feelings are mutual." Mrs. Arnoff shook her finger and Ava realized Lillian was slightly drunk.

That could make things easier.

"What did my husband want? It's just like him to send a woman to fetch for him."

Max stepped close to Ava and nudged the side of her hip. "His laptop. Isn't that what you told me, Ava? And samples, some kind of samples."

Ava nodded, the stupid smile still on her face, a breath trapped in her lungs. Max had just decided to go for it.

Lillian's brow furrowed and she tucked strands from her gray bob behind her ear. "His laptop's in his office, but I'm not sure what samples you mean. He doesn't keep any of his lab work at home."

"Let me grab the laptop first." Ava pivoted toward the hallway. "His office?"

"I'll show you."

Max cleared his throat. "Do you mind if I use your restroom?"

Ava shot him a glance beneath her lashes. Did he think he'd find the T-101 pills in the medicine cabinet?

"Right across from the office, Mike." She patted Ava's hand. "Follow us."

Lillian weaved toward the hallway and Ava got the crazy idea that if they shared a bottle of wine with her, she might just pass out.

When they reached the first two rooms in the hallway, Lillian pushed at the door on the right. "Bathroom in here."

Then she reached into the room across from the bathroom and flicked on a light. "He usually leaves his laptop on the corner of his desk. Did his computer go down at the lab or something?"

"He didn't tell me, Lillian. I just obey orders. He asks me to pick up his laptop—" she snapped her fingers "—I pick up his laptop."

"And samples?"

Ava scooped up the laptop from the desk and hugged it to her chest. "He meant the blue pills. You know, the blue pills?"

Lillian tilted her head. "He doesn't tell me much about his work. Can you email him or something and ask him where they are?"

"I-it was an afterthought. Maybe they're not very important."

Lillian led her out of the office and winked before she turned off the light. "Maybe if we forget about it, Charles will come home to get them himself."

They stepped into the hallway, and Max came from the opposite end.

"Hope you don't mind. There was no hand soap in this bathroom, so I found another."

"That's fine."

As Lillian headed back to the living room, Ava squeezed Max's hand and he shook his head. No blue pills in the medicine cabinets, but at least they got the laptop.

"Are you sure you don't want some wine?" She grabbed her glass and gulped down the remainder of the burgundy liquid. "God knows, my husband's never home anymore to join me."

"Ava, why don't you have a glass with her? If you don't mind, Lillian, I'll just take a quick look in the garage since Ava mentioned he sometimes works out there."

Mrs. Arnoff blinked her eyes. "He does?"

"Yes, yes, he did say something about storing some work in the garage." Ava swept past Lillian and grabbed a glass from the wet bar in the corner. "I'd love to join you."

The boozy smile erased the confusion from Lillian's face. "Wonderful. It's an outstanding year for this particular cab."

She almost knocked the bottle over and Ava grabbed it. "Allow me."

Max had disappeared through the door to the attached garage, and Ava poured a generous amount of wine into Lillian's glass and a splash in her own.

She clinked her glass with Lillian's. "Here's to Dr. Arnoff."

"Wherever he is." Lillian took a long pull from her glass.

The knock on the front door startled them both.

Lillian put her glass down and brushed her fingers together. "Looks like we're going to have a party tonight without Charles."

She took a halting step toward the front door as Ava glanced at the garage. If that was the police reporting Dr. Arnoff's death, she'd better do some quick thinking and she could use Max's help.

Mrs. Arnoff was halfway to the front door when Max came barreling into the room. "Don't answer that."

"What?" Lillian stumbled to a stop.

"You shouldn't answer your door when you're home alone at night."

"But I'm not alone." Lillian spread her arms to take in the two of them and proceeded to the door.

"Wait." Max held up his hand.

A man yelled from the porch. "Mrs. Arnoff? It's the cable company. Several people in your area have been reporting outages."

Ava's heart thumped and she stepped back, glancing at the TV, still flickering with images. Lillian must have a great cable provider if they came out at this time of night.

Mrs. Arnoff reached the door and placed her hand on the knob while leaning toward the peephole. She called out, "I think my TV's fine." She glanced over her shoulder at Ava. "Don't you think so?"

Max charged forward and grabbed the laptop. Then he took Ava's arm and whispered in her ear. "We need to get out of here. She just announced our presence."

"We still need to check, ma'am," the voice on the porch insisted.

Lillian took the chain off the door and Max yanked Ava toward the sliding door in the back.

As soon as Max slid open the back door, a crackling sound rang behind them and Lillian fell back into the room—missing half her head.

Chapter Eight

Ava didn't have time to react. Didn't have time to let loose with the scream gathering in her lungs.

Max yanked her out the back door and sped across the patio toward the fence on the side. She moved mechanically, still in shock. His voice grated in a harsh whisper. "I don't know if they saw us or not, but they'll know someone was there. Even if they didn't hear Lillian speaking to you, they'll notice the second wineglass."

They reached the fence and Max bent over and cupped his hands to hoist her up.

She wedged one sneakered foot in his hands and grabbed the top of the stuccoed fence. She pulled herself up and over, landing in some dirt on the other side. "Slip the laptop over."

She stepped onto a sprinkler cover and reached up with trembling hands. The hard edge of the laptop met her grasping fingers and she eased it over the wall and hugged it to her chest. "Got it."

Two seconds later, Max vaulted over the fence, landing beside her. "Any vicious beasts in residence?"

She gulped. "Not yet."

She followed his lead across the backyard, hunching forward and keeping to the shadows, her knees trembling with each step. The next fence presented a bigger problem, as spiky hedges bordered the entire length.

She huffed out a breath, as fear clawed through her chest. "How are we going to get over that fence?"

"Don't worry. We got this. The hedges are stiff enough to use as a ledge."

Before she could respond, he took the laptop from her and his hands encircled her waist. He lifted her off the ground, high into the air. "Find a stable point to get a foothold."

With her legs dangling in the air, she tapped her foot against the dense hedge until she found a stationary spot. "I think I'm good here."

"Is there a place to put your hands?"

She groped along the edge of the bush, ignoring the sharp pain from the nettles, and found the rounded top of the stucco fence that separated the two houses. "Yeah."

"Are they coming?"

Glancing across the yard, she shook her head. "I don't see anything coming this way."

He released her and she put her weight on her hands, her feet lightly dancing over the hedge until she could swing her legs over the fence. She let herself drop to the ground.

Her panting merged with the panting coming from behind her and she spun around and nearly tripped over a furry, four-legged creature.

Before she could warn Max, he dropped down beside her with the laptop tucked beneath one arm. The dog backed up, lifted his nose and let out a howl.

"Shh." Ava dropped to her knees and placed her hands on either side of the mutt's head and rubbed his ears. "You don't need to do that."

The howl ended and the little dog pranced around their feet in excitement.

Max nudged her back with his knee. "Let's get going before he changes his mind."

Rising to her feet, Ava chucked the pup under the chin, reluctant to leave the one spot of normalcy in the entire evening. "You're a good boy."

They dashed across the yard with the dog at their heels, but at least he'd decided they were friends instead of foes.

The fence on the other side, leading to the street where Max had parked the car, posed less of an obstacle than the other fence, and they both hopped over easily, landing on the sidewalk across from the stolen SUV.

Ava took a step toward the curb, but Max had other ideas. He grabbed her wrist and pulled her back.

"Hold on." He nudged her behind his back as he ventured into the street, looking both ways. "Stay with me."

She practically stepped on his heels as she jogged across the street in his wake.

When they reached the car, he cupped his hands at the window to peer inside. He nodded and carefully opened the door.

She did the same on her side and let out a long breath when she collapsed on the passenger seat. She twisted around and placed the laptop on the floor of the backseat.

Max started the car and then manually turned off the headlights that came on automatically. He put the car in Reverse and backed up, avoiding Dr. Arnoff's street.

It didn't do any good.

Just when he reached the next cross street, a car, its headlights blinding them, came roaring around the corner.

Max didn't miss a beat. The Tempest agents must've gone out to the street, listening to every sound in the night—the howl of the dog and the engine of the car. He continued his reverse turn around the block, and when the other car turned down the same block, Max punched the accelerator and sped past the car in the other direction.

His eyes darted to the side mirror. The driver of the other car hadn't bothered turning around. He'd taken off after them in Reverse. That gave him and Ava an advantage.

Max clenched the steering wheel. Now if he only had a high-performance car instead of this clunky SUV. They were fast approaching the end of the block, and he'd have to make a hard right turn or end up in someone's living room.

He glanced at Ava's white face. "Hang on."

The other car was almost abreast of them. Max eased off the accelerator and jerked the steering wheel to the right. The tires squealed but stayed on the road—for the most part.

Cranking her head around, Ava peered between the two front seats and out the back window. "They made the turn. Now they're facing the right direction."

"That's good. Now they can go even faster."

"How is that good? They're going to catch up to us."

"I noticed something on that first road we turned on just off the freeway. I was cursing this SUV a few seconds ago, but I think its wide body is just what we need."

"If you say so. Are they going to start shooting into this car?"

"If they get the chance." With the other car roaring closely behind them, Max kept floating to the left to keep them from drawing up next to them. But he had plans to take them to a wider stretch, as long as they didn't start taking potshots at the back of the SUV.

He careened around the next corner toward the freeway, keeping the SUV in the middle of the road so the other driver couldn't see what was on the horizon.

When Max neared the dip in the road that he'd noticed before, he slowed the SUV until the other car was almost at their bumper. Then he pulled to the right and slammed on the brakes.

The black sedan screamed past them and hit the dip going almost seventy. The front end of the car flew into the air, its spinning wheels leaving the asphalt. It seemed to float for a second and then crashed to earth with the shrill sound of twisting metal. Max saw a single wheel go airborne before he headed down another street for the freeway.

A siren wailed in the distance and Ava pressed her hands to her heart. "Someone had already called the police."

"Too bad there are no witnesses to the crash since we'll be long gone. I wonder if the cops are going to discover Mrs. Arnoff's body?"

Ava pinned her hands between her knees. "I'm slowing you down, aren't I? They wouldn't have tracked us down if I hadn't used my ATM card like an idiot."

"Don't keep beating yourself up about that. You're a civilian. Your mind doesn't work like mine. I should've known Tempest would pay a visit to Mrs. Arnoff—just didn't realize they'd show up so soon and kill her."

"You did know they'd pay her a visit, but in the end it was worth the risk, wasn't it?" She jerked her thumb at the backseat. "We got Arnoff's laptop."

"That's another thing. I never would've known about that laptop, Ava."

She sighed and tilted her head back. "What now?"

"We need to take a look at Arnoff's computer, see if he has any information about an antidote or the location of more blue pills."

"Even looking at his notes on the serum will help us, help me. I just might be able to figure out a way to neutralize the drug's effects."

"And I need to warn the other Tempest agents."

He could feel her gaze searching his face.

"Why do you need to do that?"

"Tempest is planning something big. All of my assignments have been leading to something big. If Simon hadn't gone off the rails like he did, I'd still be working for Tempest, still be on the inside."

"You still wouldn't have gotten all the names of the other agents. Tempest kept you apart, right?"

"That's right, unless we worked an assignment together like Simon and I did. My guess is Tempest won't be putting any agents together anymore. Anyway, I'm hoping to get the other agents' names from Arnoff's laptop, unless you have their names."

"I just knew a few names, usually first names only. Most of my patients didn't want to get personal."

He slid a quick glance her way. He'd wanted to get personal with her even though she'd known them by their numbers. "They may have given you phony names anyway."

"Did you and Simon discuss your memory lapses and suspicions when you had that assignment together?"

"Not then, but we became aware of each other. Later he found me in Brussels. I don't know how he found me and I don't know how he knew I was having the same experiences he was having, unless it was something he noticed during that joint assignment."

"Did you ever ask him?"

"Of course I did. He wouldn't tell me. I don't know if it was for his safety or mine."

"Or someone else's."

He raised an eyebrow. "You think he had someone on the inside?"

She shrugged. "Where are we going?"

"We're going to drive for a while and find a place to spend the night. Then we're going to delve into the private world of Dr. Charles Arnoff."

He bypassed the lights of Albuquerque and headed toward a small town on its outskirts. He'd need to swap this car for another. He had the cash to buy a used car and avoid the danger of getting pulled over for auto theft.

Ava tapped on the window. "How about that place? Not too small, not too big."

"Why don't we want a small motel?"

"Too few people checking in, so we'd be more memorable."

"And why not too big?"

"Too crowded, so we wouldn't be able to keep track of the other guests coming and going." She tilted her head. "Was that a test?"

"If you're going to help me out for a little while longer, I need to prepare you better."

"But you did tell me not to use my cards. I wasn't listening to the subtext of your words."

"You shouldn't have to listen for subtext—this is life and death. I'm going to spell it out for you from now on."

From now on? He took the next turn a little too fast. Ava could help him figure out what was on Arnoff's computer, and then she needed to get out of here—away from him.

He swiped the back of his hand across the beads of sweat on his upper lip.

"The pills?" She hunched forward in her seat, her brow furrowed.

"Yeah, I could use another, but I'm going to try to hold out."

"You're not going to hold out as long as you did yesterday. That's just dangerous."

"It'll be dangerous when I run out of the meds, too."

"That's not going to happen."

He swung into the parking lot of the midsize motel. The night clerk was talking to another guest when they walked into the lobby.

Max sized up the other man with a glance—tourist looking to escape his room filled with the wife and kids.

Although he had some cards with an alternate ID, Max repeated his bankruptcy story and the clerk was only too happy to take cash.

"The luck's with you tonight. We have two rooms left and both have a king-size bed."

"Great." He'd be spending the night on the floor.

Max handed over the cash and the clerk slid two key cards across the counter. "Enjoy your stay."

Ava tapped her card against her chin. "Free Wi-Fi?"

"Yes, ma'am."

They left the clerk and the guest to their conversation and headed for the side door that led to their room. Steam rose from the outdoor pool and Jacuzzi to their right, and heads bobbed above the gurgling water.

Max rolled his shoulders. "That looks inviting about now."

"Tell me about it." Ava rubbed her head.

He stopped and placed his hands on her shoulders. "Are you okay? That was a wild car ride and you must've gotten jostled around. I'm sorry I didn't even ask if you were hurt."

Her lashes fluttered as her chest rose and fell quickly. The pulse in her throat beat out her scent, and it was as intoxicating as the bougainvillea creeping along the gate surrounding the pool.

"I—I'm fine. I didn't think we were going to get out of there alive."

He gave her shoulders a squeeze before releasing them. "Too bad they heard Mrs. Arnoff talking to us before she opened the door. We could've gotten away and they would've never known we were there."

"Too bad Lillian opened the door at all. She'd still be alive."

"No, she wouldn't be, Ava." He turned back to the lit pathway, and she followed him silently.

He told her he was going to be truthful, and that meant making sure she knew the tenacity of the enemy they faced. Tempest came to do a job and Mrs. Arnoff's death was the goal of that job. Finding him and Ava there had just been a bonus.

They reached their room, and Max opened the door for Ava, pushing it wide. The big bed dominated the space, but Max did his best to ignore it.

He dropped his bag in the corner. "You must be starving. I noticed a pizza place a few doors down. I'm sure they deliver here."

"That sounds fine." She parked the laptop on the credenza next to the TV and placed her suitcase next to his duffel. "Should we start in with the laptop?"

"Let's get some food in first. It might take some work to get around Dr. Arnoff's security." He reached into the front pocket of his jeans and shook the tin back and forth, tumbling the pills inside. "Besides, I've got four pills left. We have plenty of time."

She rolled her eyes at him. "Is that your attempt at humor?"

"Not very funny, huh?" He tossed the tin onto the nightstand.

"Don't give up your day job."

"Now, *that's* funny." He yanked open the single drawer of the nightstand and pulled out a telephone book. "Pizza, pizza. Here it is. We're on Cochise Road, right?"

She perched on the edge of the bed, reached across him and plucked up the notepad next to the phone. "Yep, Cochise Road."

He held the receiver of the phone to his ear. "What do you want? The works?"

"Excluding anchovies and pineapple." She wrinkled her nose, looking adorable, and *adorable* wasn't a word he used often—ever.

He ordered the pizza and then pulled some change from his pocket. He jingled it in his palm. "I saw a vending machine out by the pool. Do you want something to drink?"

"Diet anything."

His gaze swept her lithe frame from head to toe. "Because you look like you need to diet."

"When you're short, you always need to watch what you consume."

"You're the doctor."

"Not really."

Her solemn voice and downturned lips had him taking two steps toward her and brushing her jawline with his fingertips. "You were the best damned doctor I ever had."

"I was injecting you with poison, and I didn't even know it. Some doctor."

"You had a great bedside manner when you were doing it." He tugged on one wavy lock of her dark brown hair, and she flashed him a quick smile from her tremulous lips.

"Lock the door behind me and don't open it for anyone. The pizza's not going to get here that fast."

"Got it."

He stood outside the door of the motel room until he heard the dead bolt and the chain. Then he followed the path back to the gated pool with a whistle on his lips.

He hadn't felt this hopeful in a long time— not since he and Simon had figured out what Tempest was doing to its agents. He finally had someone on his side—someone who offered real help, not a hothead like Simon.

What had Ava done to lose her chance at a medical license? He couldn't imagine her doing something illegal, although she hadn't been squeamish about stealing cars and lying to Lillian Arnoff. In fact, she'd adapted to life on the run more quickly than he would've imagined.

He braced a hand against the soda machine outside the pool gate and studied the selections. A woman's low laugh bubbled from the hot tub, followed by a soft squeal and a sigh.

He closed his eyes. He'd like to try to make Ava sigh like that—a sigh of contentment instead of one of exhaustion or fear.

His lids flew open, and he fed some coins in the slot and punched the button for a diet soda and then repeated the process for a root beer. He'd try to get a good night's sleep tonight and pop one of the precious pills in the morning.

Gripping a cold can in each hand, he glanced over his shoulder at the steam rising from the hot tub, the heads so close together now as to be indistinguishable. Lucky bastard.

When he returned to the room, he tapped on the door with the edge of one can. "It's me."

She slipped the chain from the door and opened it.

"I hope you looked out that peephole before opening the door."

"I did, although that didn't help Mrs. Arnoff, did it?"

"Mrs. Arnoff was a fool—and drunk. A bad combination."

She took her soda from his hand. "She paid a high price for a few glasses of wine."

"She paid a high price for being married to

Dr. Arnoff." He slammed the door behind him and threw the chain in place again. "And you're paying a high price for working with the man."

"Maybe Dr. Arnoff didn't realize how Tempest was using its agents. Maybe he truly thought you were a force for good."

"Then why all the secrecy? Why keep you out of the loop?"

"That's easy." She popped the tab on her can and bubbles sprayed from the lid. "What he was doing was completely unethical. T-101 hadn't been properly tested or vetted or reviewed or approved by the FDA. It was a dream situation for Dr. Arnoff. Tempest was funding an illegal lab for him, a lab where he had complete control."

"And unwitting guinea pigs at his disposal."

Ava wandered to the laptop on the credenza. "I powered it up while you were gone. It's password-protected and there's not much life left on the battery."

"We're going to have to crack that password." A pulse pounded in his temple, making his eye twitch.

"And we're going to have to get a new power cord."

"How much juice does it have left?" He rubbed his eye with his fist.

"About an hour, and I just might be able to figure out that password."

"How are you going to do that?" He dropped into the one chair in the room, stationed by the sliding door that led to a small patio.

A rosy pink blush rushed across her cheeks. "I went through Dr. Arnoff's desk once at the lab."

"Really?" He cocked one eyebrow at her. Definitely not as sweet as she appeared.

She spread out her hands. "It was because of the lab. He was so secretive, I decided to do a little digging of my own."

"You obviously didn't dig very far if you didn't find out the real purpose behind T-101."

"No, I never did get that far, but I did discover a bunch of his passwords. There's a good reason why cyber security people advise against writing down your passwords."

He pointed at the computer. "Have you tried any of them yet? Do you even remember them?"

"I remember some of them. I'd just tried a few when you knocked on the door, but I was afraid of draining the battery."

Another knock sounded on the door, and Max held up one finger. "Hang on."

He squinted through the peephole while grabbing the door handle. "It's pizza time."

Still, he felt for his weapon tucked into his holster before opening the door. Anyone could impersonate a pizza delivery guy, just like anyone could impersonate a cable repairman.

The pizza guy held the box in front of him. "Pizza?"

"That's us. How much do I owe you?"

"That's fifteen ninety-five."

Max traded a twenty for the pizza. "Keep it. Thanks."

"Thank you."

Max locked up again and put the pizza on the credenza next to the laptop. "Do you want to try again?"

"My mind is in a fog right now, and I don't want to waste the battery trying out twenty different passwords. I'd rather wait for that power cord."

He tapped the box. "Sit down and have a slice or two before you faint from hunger." Or was he the only one ravenous?

Ava looked around the room. "Our seating options are limited, aren't they?"

"You can have the chair. I'll take the bed."

"Just don't leave any crumbs in there."

He could've said something about crumbs in the bed and whether or not he'd kick her out for the offense, but he refrained. She obviously hadn't considered the sleeping arrangements yet.

He dropped two pieces of pizza on one of the

paper plates provided by the pizzeria and handed it to Ava. "Looks good."

Then he filled up his own plate and reclined on the bed against a couple of pillows. The cool pillow felt soothing against the back of his head, which had started throbbing, along with his temple, in the past ten minutes.

Had to be hunger. He tore into a slice of pizza with his teeth. The flavor of the spicy pepperoni filled his mouth, and he wiped his chin with a napkin.

Ava took a small bite from the tip of the triangle and dabbed her lips. "Mmm, that hit the spot."

He waved his pizza at her. "You *are* going to eat more, right?"

"Of course." Her gaze slid to the computer on the credenza. "I'm dying to find out what's on there."

"It's almost eleven o'clock, Ava. We're not going to find a power cord at this time of night. We can pick up a cord first thing tomorrow."

"You have a point." She leaned forward and closed the lid of the laptop. Then she collapsed back in the chair and took a big bite of her pizza.

"Are you going to tell me how Tempest recruited you?"

He dropped his crust on the plate and brushed his fingers together, trying to buy time.

"The short answer?"

"Do you have any other kind?"

"I was a Green Beret, and I disobeyed orders. Tempest saved me from a court-martial."

"D-did you do something wrong? Something illegal?"

"I saved four men in my unit." His mouth twisted. "But I still disobeyed orders. They were bad orders."

"Tempest must've been on the lookout for guys like you."

"Yep."

"Where's your family? Do they know you're going through this?"

"That's another thing Tempest looks out for—I have no family."

"Parents, siblings?"

"I was an only child and my parents died in an embassy bombing in Africa. My dad was with the State Department."

"I'm sorry."

"That's why I enlisted." He rose from the bed and placed two more pizza slices on his plate. "I didn't tell you my sob story to ruin your appetite. Eat up."

She nibbled at the edges of her second piece of pizza. "Did you go into the service with the intention of saving the world or just avenging the deaths of your parents?"

"Does it matter? It led me to the same place."

"I never knew all this about you when you were my patient."

"It's not something I'm going to blurt out to a medical doctor."

"Stop calling me that." She took a fast gulp of soda and her eyes watered.

"You know it's coming, don't you, Ava?"

She looked up from wiping her eyes with a napkin. "What?"

"How did Dr. Arnoff recruit you? I showed you mine, and now you definitely have to show me yours."

The pink tide rushed into her cheeks once again.

He hadn't meant that as a sexual reference, but if she'd taken it that way then maybe this attraction he felt for her wasn't one-sided.

She tossed the napkin onto her plate and folded her hands in her lap. "While I was still in medical school, a clinical student, my brother thought it was a good idea to use my credentials to steal meds and write prescriptions."

"Addict?"

"Yes, just like our father before him."

"How did his actions impact you? I can see reprimanding you for carelessness or poor judgment, but you didn't steal the stuff."

The knuckles of her laced fingers turned

white, and she clamped her lower lip between her teeth.

"Did you?"

"I didn't steal anything...but they thought I did."

"Because you let them believe it." He rolled the can between his palms. "You took the fall for your brother."

"I had to. He was facing his third strike." Her chin jutted forward, and her lips thinned out to a straight line. "He has an illness, and he was not going to be let off with a slap on the wrist and a treatment plan."

"So, you allowed him to ruin your career and everything you'd worked for?"

"It's complicated." She rose from the chair and wedged her shoulder against the sliding glass door. "Our parents were a mess. Mom crashed her car into a tree while driving drunk and Dad dealt with the loss of his drinking partner by ingesting even more drugs before OD'ing. Even before they died, I'd always taken care of Cody. I guess I didn't do a very good job."

"Because raising a child is not the job for another child." He plumped the pillows behind him and massaged his temples. "Where is your brother now?"

She traced a pattern on the window with her fingertip. "He's in Utah, working at one of the

ski resorts near Salt Lake as a snowboard instructor. I think he's tending bar until all the lifts
are open up there."

"Did he even feel a shred of guilt letting you
take the fall? Did he ever make any kind of res-
titution?"

"Sure he did." A half smile curved her lip.
"He hooked me up with Dr. Arnoff."

A shaft of pain flashed behind his eyes, and
he squeezed them shut.

"Are you okay?"

"Slight headache." He pinched the bridge of
his nose. "Your brother knew Dr. Arnoff?"

"He'd met him on a hike in the Grand Can-
yon." She turned to face him, leaning her back
against the glass of the door. "Cody didn't tell
me at the time, but he and Dr. Arnoff had shared
some hallucinogens."

His eyes flew open, his brows jumping. "Dr.
Arnoff was into psychedelics?"

"Dr. Arnoff was into experimentation. Anyway, when Cody told Dr. Arnoff about me, the
doctor said he might have a job for me at his lab.
The rest—" she spread her hands "—is history."

"That's gotta be the weirdest job referral ever."

"Yeah, and look where it got me." She pushed
off the door and folded her plate in half. "All
kinds of alarms were going off in my head after
I spoke to Dr. Arnoff, but I ignored every last

one of them. I just wanted to see patients, treat people. I allowed that desire to override my common sense."

"I get it, Ava."

"You would." She buzzed around the napkins and packets of cheese, ending her confessional.

He did get it—and her. No wonder Tempest had targeted them both.

He forced his heavy limbs off the bed and helped her clean up. "Do you want the rest of the pizza?"

"We can have it for breakfast."

"My kinda girl."

He just wished he didn't mean that so literally. He'd always looked forward to seeing Ava at the clinic, and spending this time with her under dire conditions had strengthened that attraction even more for some crazy reason.

He coughed. "Do you want to use the bathroom first?"

"Sure."

While Ava was in the bathroom, he dropped a couple of pillows on the floor and found an extra blanket in the closet. He'd set up a serviceable place to sleep by the time she finished brushing her teeth.

She exited the bathroom with a hitch in her step. "What's that?"

"My bed for the night."

Her gaze shifted to the real bed. "You can have the bed. You were just complaining about a headache. You take it. That blanket isn't even going to cover your feet."

"I've slept on a lot worse."

"I'm sure you have, Max, but that's not the point." She stuffed her clothes in her suitcase and perched on the edge of the bed in the long cotton T-shirt she'd bought for a nightgown. "If you won't trade, then just join me. This bed is big enough for the two of us."

His pulse thudded thickly in his throat. "I don't want to crowd you."

"I don't take up a lot of room, and I wouldn't be able to sleep knowing you were on the hard floor."

"It's not that bad." He tapped his foot on the blanket.

"Max."

"Okay, you don't have to twist my arm. Pick your side and I'll hit the bathroom."

After he brushed his teeth, he braced his hands on the sink and leaned into the mirror. He had no intention of making a move on Ava, but sleeping next to her just might drive him crazier than the lack of T-101. With any luck, she'd be sound asleep by the time he made it back to the bedroom.

He stripped to his boxers and then considered

putting his T-shirt back on. He could always sleep on top of the covers with that blanket he'd found in the closet.

He turned off the light and eased open the door to the room. He could barely discern Ava's small frame on the far side of the bed, lying on her side, the covers pulled up to her nose.

The lamp on his side of the bed still burned, and he crept across the carpeted floor and placed his folded clothes on top of his bag. On his way to the bed, he snatched up the blanket and pillows from the floor and settled on top of the covers, wrapping the blanket around his body.

Ava couldn't be sleeping over there with that shallow breathing, but her pretense was probably a good thing.

He closed his eyes and tried to block out the images that always marched across his mind at night. He had no way of knowing which ones were real or fake anyway.

A sliver of pain lanced his temple. He'd hoped to put off taking a pill until morning, since that would mean progress.

A bead of sweat rolled down his face, and he licked his dry lips. He'd left the tin of pills on the nightstand and tried to raise his arm to reach them, but the familiar numbness invaded his limbs.

The pictures in his head flashed like a slide

show across his vision, and his hands curled into fists. The blood. The carnage. The destruction.

A strangled cry rose from his throat. A surge of adrenaline reanimated him. He clawed the blanket from his body.

He had to make them stop. He reached for the form next to him and sank his fingers into the soft skin.

Chapter Nine

Max's hand grabbed the back of her neck. Already on alert, she twisted away from him and shouted his name.

She tumbled from the bed and landed on the floor with a thud.

The thrashing and moaning continued from the bed, so she crawled on the floor around the foot of it. He'd tossed the blue pills on the nightstand.

She reached up from the floor and plucked the tin from the bedside table. She popped it open and pinched one of the pills between her thumb and forefinger.

She turned her attention to Max, his limbs flailing, frightening, guttural sounds emanating from his lips. The same sounds Simon had been making.

She let out a long breath and hopped onto the bed. "Max. Max, listen to me."

His head thrashed to the side, and she straddled his body, clutching the pill.

"Max, it's Ava. I'm going to put this pill beneath your tongue. You'll be fine in a few minutes."

Did his dark eyes gleam with understanding from the pain etched across his face?

She slipped her fingers inside his mouth and tucked the pill beneath his tongue, covering his lips with one hand.

He bucked beneath her, his hands cinching her around the waist. Another minute. "C'mon, Max. You can do it. It's me. It's reality. You're coming back."

His frame lost its rigidity. He pulled in a couple of long breaths. He blinked and swallowed. "Ava."

Despite the raspy edge, it was the sweetest sound she'd ever heard. Leaning forward, she cupped his jaw with her hand. "That's right. It's Ava. I'm here."

The hands around her waist tightened before they dropped.

His spiky, dark lashes shuttered his eyes, and he dragged the back of his hand across his mouth. "Did I...did I hurt you?"

Her heart pounded. "Absolutely not. I wasn't in any danger at all."

He cursed and shifted her off his body. "I could've killed you."

Lying next to him, she didn't move one muscle. "I don't believe that, Max."

He sat up and shook his head, his chest heaving with every breath. "I should've taken another pill when we ate. I had no right to push my luck—not with you here."

"It's a good thing I was here. I was able to do something for you this time."

"I haven't done anything for you except drag you into a mess of epic proportions."

"You've saved me so many times, I'm beginning to lose count, and you didn't drag me into anything. I walked into this mess with my eyes wide open. I posed as a doctor and worked for a man I already knew to be unethical."

He rolled out of bed—away from her—and stumbled toward the credenza. He grabbed a bottle of water and chugged the contents.

"Now, I'm going to spend the rest of the night on the floor, and if you had an ounce of sense, you'd sneak out of here while I'm asleep."

For the first time in a long time, something made perfect sense to her. She whipped back the covers on the bed and patted the mattress. "You need a good night's sleep now more than ever, and the floor is not going to cut it."

He hesitated halfway to the bed, folding his arms over the sculpted chest she couldn't help noticing.

"I mean it, Duvall. Doctor's orders, even if they're from a fake doctor. Get back to bed and relax. You have a small dosage of T-101 running through your veins. No chance of another seizure now."

He snorted. "Is that what you're calling it?"

But at least he was moving toward the bed—and her.

He crawled in beside her and she let out a pent-up breath. "Feeling better?"

"Anything's better than what I just went through." He held his hands in front of him and flexed his fingers. "I could've hurt you."

"You didn't."

He turned away from her and shifted to his side.

Did he think he could get rid of her that easily?

She rolled to her side facing his back and stroked the hair away from his forehead. "It's going to be okay, Max. You're going to be okay."

And she would be okay as long as she had this damaged man to protect her. Then she would return the favor—she was going to fix Max Duvall.

THE WARM SKIN felt smooth beneath her fingertips. Ava moved in closer and rested her cheek against Max's broad back as she brushed her knuckles across the hard plates of muscle on his chest.

She'd examined his beautiful body, scars and all, at the clinic before, but never in such an intimate way. She uncurled her hand and ran her palm up to his shoulder.

He sighed and halfway rolled onto his back, flinging his arm to the side where it rested across her hip.

She took his hand in hers and smoothed her fingertips over the rough spots where his fingers met his palm. They had to make this right. He could keep lowering his dosage, but an antidote would counteract the drug's effects in his system. Arnoff had to have one somewhere.

"What time is it?"

His gruff voice startled her, and she dropped his hand. "Sorry."

He shifted completely to his back and stretched his arms over his head. "For what?"

She held up her hands, spreading her fingers. "For mauling you in your sleep."

He hitched up to his elbows. "If that was mauling, I'm all for it."

"How are you feeling?"

"Okay." He ran his tongue over his teeth. "Dry mouth, slight headache, but I still have my sanity—thanks to you."

"All I did was give you a pill." She tugged the hem of her T-shirt over her thighs.

"That's all I needed."

"You need that antidote."

"Yeah, that too."

She sat up and tilted her chin toward Dr. Arnoff's laptop. "And we just might find the clues to that antidote in there."

"I'm claiming the shower first, and then I'll go out and pick up some breakfast. Bagels, coffee?"

"Anything like that." Max had just put an end to her visions of lolling in bed with him while they discussed strategy. Who was she kidding? If he wanted her, he could've had her. She'd had her hands all over him. Wasn't that obvious enough for him?

The slam of the bathroom door put a punctuation mark on her foolish imaginings.

She scooted off the bed and flipped the lid on the laptop. Sleep had recharged her brain if not the battery, and she had recalled several different letter, number and character combinations that Arnoff had written down using his wife's name. She'd give those a try and then wait for the power cord.

She powered on the computer, checking the battery life. Looked as though they had about an hour—an hour to save a life.

She wrote down each password as she tried it and then squealed when she entered the fifth combination.

Max charged out of the bathroom, sluicing his

long hair back from his face, his jeans hanging low on his hips. "Are you okay out here?"

"More than okay. I got the password."

"I'm impressed, especially after the night you just had."

The night she'd just had was her best in recent memory. "I recalled that he'd written down his wife's name using different letters, numbers and characters. It just took a few tries, but we're still going to need that power cord."

"We can at least make a start." He rubbed his knuckles across the dark stubble on his chin. "I was thinking in the shower, Ava."

Her gaze flicked to his flat belly and back to his face. "I'm listening."

"If we can't locate any more blue pills or an antidote in the next few days, I want you gone."

She tapped the computer's keyboard. "We're going to find something, Max. Dr. Arnoff may have been unethical, but he was brilliant. He wouldn't have developed a drug like T-101 without an escape plan."

"You find that escape plan while I go round up some breakfast." He pulled a T-shirt over his head, strapped on his shoulder holster and shrugged into a jacket. He turned at the door. "Lock up behind me and don't answer for anyone."

She padded to the door after it closed and put

the locks and chain in place. Then she picked up the pad of paper with the hotel logo on it and dragged the chair in front of the computer on the credenza.

She wrote down the names of all the folders on the desktop, arranged them in alphabetical order and double clicked on the first one.

She was into the third folder by the time Max returned with breakfast. She opened the door wide as he walked through with coffee in each hand and a white bag pinned to his side with his elbow.

"Nothing fancy—just a couple of bagels with some cream cheese and coffee. I did throw some sugars and creams in the bag."

She pointed to the coffee cups. "Are these the same?"

"Plain old black coffee."

"Fine with me once I douse it with cream."

She popped the lid on her coffee and dumped in three little containers of cream. "I'm systematically going through the files on the desktop. I haven't even opened the hard drive yet to see what's on there."

"Discover anything so far?" He ripped into the bag and twisted two halves of a bagel apart.

"Nothing, but I'm only on the third of seven folders."

"I'll help you as soon as I devour this bagel. In

fact—" he reached out and hooked a finger beneath the sleeve of her nightshirt "—why don't you take a shower and get dressed and let me take over folder duty."

Her cheeks burned as she glanced down at the hem of her T-shirt where it hit her midthigh. "I completely forgot."

"I know. You couldn't wait to delve into that computer." He licked some cream cheese from his thumb. "What am I looking for?"

"Formulas, calculations, numbers, any reference to T-101."

"Agents' names."

"Yeah, that too." She shoved the laptop in his direction. "I'll make myself presentable."

He grunted and started tapping at the keyboard, which was not the response she'd been fishing for.

Max didn't play those games. He dealt in black and white, not subtleties.

She dug through her suitcase for clean clothes and retreated to the bathroom. This morning she washed her hair and scrubbed her body to remove all traces of Max that still clung to her from spending the night in the same bed with him. If someone had told her a month ago that she and Max Duvall would sleep in the same bed and actually sleep, she would've sent them to have their head examined.

She toweled off her hair and scrunched up her waves with some mousse on her hands. She pulled on the same jeans from yesterday, a white camisole and a blue V-neck sweater over it. She stroked on a little makeup and even added a swipe of lipstick. Just because Max didn't actually voice his compliments, it didn't mean he didn't notice.

She stepped from the bathroom and folded her nightshirt on top of her suitcase. "Find anything?"

"I'm not as methodical as you, but I may have located some of the other agents. I entered the names I knew in the search engine, and they pop up in a few places."

"While I understand your desire to warn the other agents, it's more important right now for you to get an antidote flowing through your veins." She hooked her thumbs in the front pockets of her jeans and sauntered to the credenza.

He lifted one shoulder. "I didn't know what to enter in the search field for a formula or antidote. I entered what I knew."

"Okay, then." She leaned over his shoulder and peered at the screen. "What came up?"

He jabbed his finger at the display. "They come up in a database in some program, but I'm not sure how to launch it. It's not some static file. It updates automatically."

"Let me see if it looks familiar." She wedged her hip on the arm of his chair, hunching forward. "Okay, I think we can open it with this database program."

She clicked on a menu and selected the icon for the program. It launched a map of the world and she opened the file with the agents' names Max had found from inside the program.

Red dots began flashing on the screen. A man's face would appear and then zoom to a different area of the map.

She held her breath as the dots populated the map, and Max swore softly.

"It's some kind of locator for the agents."

When the last dot found its home, Ava expelled a long breath. "Are you on here?"

"I didn't see myself." He poked at the middle of New Mexico. "And there's nothing coming up in our location."

"How is this program tracking agents?"

"I'm not sure. I'm just relieved Tempest didn't inject some kind of tracker beneath my skin. I'd been worried about that."

"Have you gotten rid of anything issued by Tempest?"

"A few things, most notably my phone. Tempest could've easily put a tracking device in our phones. We're supposed to carry them with us at all times. They have a hotline to Tempest and not much else." He flicked a finger at the map somewhere south of them. "But this is what I'm interested in. This looks like the agent closest to us—somewhere in Central America."

"Wait. Click on the red dot so we can see who it is."

Max clicked on the dot, and a head shot appeared on the screen with a name.

"You know him?"

"That's Malcolm Snyder, or at least that's the name he gave me. He's very quiet, almost shy. Are you going to try to track him down?"

"My goal is to get to all of them, help all of them break free."

She laid her hand over his on the mouse. "You need to break free first, Max. You can't save every Tempest agent unless you save yourself."

"I know that, which is why we'll keep looking through Arnoff's files. We may have to venture onto the next big town so we can buy a power cord for the laptop. I don't think the local hardware store is going to have one."

"Looks like we have another half hour or so." She tugged on his arm. "Let me get on there. If we're not following my system, I might as well start searching for some common formulas."

They switched places, and he pulled another bagel from the bag. "Do you want one?"

"You take it." As the laptop's battery drained, she started typing more furiously. Every action seemed like a race against time—if not the battery, then the blue pills. What would happen to Max when he ran out? To save his life, he might have to throw himself on Tempest's mercy. He wouldn't allow himself to go down the same road as Simon—possibly hurting other people, possibly hurting her.

She glanced over her shoulder at him lounging across the bed, biting into a bagel and watching a football game on TV. Would he take himself out rather than submitting to Tempest again? She shivered and slurped a sip of lukewarm coffee.

She entered another chemical from Dr. Arnoff's original T-101 formula and clicked on Search. Three files popped up and she sucked in a breath.

"I got a hit here."

He muted the TV and joined her at the credenza.

"This chemical is in the original formula." She opened the first file and the formula for T-101 was laid out on the screen. Her pulse rate ticked up. "We're onto something."

"You're onto something. That looks like gobbledygook to me."

"Very important gobbledygook." She minimized the file and opened the next one. Her gaze darted down the screen, and she squealed and grabbed Max's arm. "I think this is it. I think this is the formula for the antidote."

He squinted at the letters and numbers against the white background. "What's that going to do for us?"

"Max—" she bounced in the seat "—this is the antidote. You can take one dose of this and it will counter effect the T-101 in your body—no blue pills, no more shots. You're done."

He scratched the sexy stubble on his chin. "It's just a formula on a computer. How do we actually get the antidote?"

She shoved back from the credenza as a low-battery message flashed across the screen. "We make it."

"You can make—" his finger circled the air in front of the computer screen "—that."

"I know how to mix a formula. I know what these chemicals are. I was allowed to do that work with Dr. Arnoff, and I've done it before in other labs."

"Yeah, but you had an actual lab. Where are you going to cook up that stuff now? In the sink at the Desert Sun Motel?"

She jumped up from the chair and paced the

floor. "I know who can find me a lab—and those chemicals."

His voice rose. "Really? Who?"

"My brother."

Chapter Ten

Max folded his arms, his rising excitement extinguished by Ava's words, which acted like a splash of cold water. "Your brother? The guy who completely screwed up your life?"

"My brother the druggie. My brother, who has dabbled in the production of meth and probably knows about every meth lab in the southwestern corner of the United States."

"A meth lab? You're going to cook up a batch of T-101 antidote in a meth lab?"

"Exactly."

"You can't trust your brother, and you can't trust anyone who cooks meth." Hadn't she learned that lesson about trust the hard way? He balled his fists against his sides. Obviously not, since she was still here with him.

"Who said anything about trust?" She waved her fingers in the air as if she was sprinkling fairy dust. "We rent the lab, cook up our own batch of drugs and leave it the way we found it."

"You said your brother's in Utah?"

"That's right. I know he'll help us. Cody owes me."

Max dragged a hand through his hair. "That Tempest agent we located on the computer is in the other direction—south."

She stopped pacing and marched toward him. She grabbed his arms with surprising force. "Unless that other agent has a storehouse of blue pills that he can share, it's pointless to warn him. We need to stabilize you first. I don't care about any Tempest agent right now except Max Duvall."

With her flushed cheeks and bright eyes, Ava looked ready to take on the world—for him. He reached out and brushed his thumb across her smooth cheek. "Why *do* you care, Ava? Am I another homeless dog to save? Another broken family member?"

Her words came out on a whisper, her warm, sweet breath caressing his throat. "You saved me. You're protecting me, and I'm going to do the same for you. Right now, you're all I have, a-and I think I'm all you have."

His thumb traced her bottom lip. "You are."

She met his gaze steadily and something passed between them—a pact, a bond. At that moment, he knew he'd do anything to protect this woman. He'd already killed for her...and he'd die for her. But not yet.

"Can you reach your brother?"

She blinked and nodded. "Yes. Should I call him now or track him down when we get to Utah? I know which resort he's working at."

"You know your brother best. Is he going to bolt if he knows you're on your way?"

"No, but I'm afraid to use my cell phone. Once I used my ATM card and they tracked us down, it got me thinking about other methods they could use to get to us. You said yourself, the program on Dr. Arnoff's laptop is probably tracking the agents through their cell phones."

He kissed her mouth because he couldn't help himself anymore and then chucked her beneath the chin. "I'm going to turn you into a covert ops agent yet. Dump your cell phone, pick up one of those temporary ones or use mine and then call your brother."

Stepping back from him, she said, "I'll get a phone at the same place where we buy a power cord for Arnoff's computer."

"We have at least a ten-hour drive ahead of us, so let's get going."

"What are we going to do about that SUV? Even if nobody saw us careening through Dr. Arnoff's neighborhood last night, the owner has definitely reported the car stolen."

"I have a bottomless pit of cash and a few fake ID's that I haven't even used yet. I'm going to purchase a car at a used-car lot, so we can drive to Utah in relative safety."

"That would be a first." Ava pivoted away from him and started shoving clothes into her bag, her long hair creating a veil over her face.

He eyed her stiff shoulders. He shouldn't have kissed her. No, the kiss was okay, but he shouldn't have made light of it after. If he'd never kissed her in the first place, he wouldn't have had to shrug it off.

Damn it. Being a robot had been a hell of a lot easier than dealing with these human emotions.

He strode across the room toward her, and she made a surprised half turn at his approach. He pulled her into his arms and planted a kiss on her parted lips.

Running his hands through her hair, he tilted her head and deepened the kiss.

One hand still clutching a T-shirt, she wrapped her arms around his waist and pressed her body against his.

The pressure of her soft breasts and intoxicating scent lit a fire in his belly. He hadn't felt this way in a long time, if ever. Tempest had tried to steal those memories from him, as well, and had mostly succeeded. Had he ever loved a woman? Did he even know how?

Was it fair to use Ava as his guinea pig?

He pulled away and dropped a kiss on her

forehead, her cheek and her nose, ignoring the stab of guilt that twisted in his gut at her confused expression. "We'd better go trade that SUV for something legal."

"Good idea."

He turned and she grabbed his hand. "Max?"

"Yeah?" Her deep green eyes drew his gaze like a magnet.

"I don't regret that kiss. Do you?"

"No."

With that single word, her face brightened and he left it at that. She didn't need to know about the confusing emotions warring in his brain right now.

Ava was a big girl and had been making her own choices for years. He couldn't help it if they'd all been bad.

Ava leaned against the headrest of the compact car as Max drove it off the used-car lot. That had been easier than she expected, but then, Max did have a boatload of cash and a few alternate identities.

He should just use one of those to get out of the country—after she injected him with some T-101 antidote. Maybe he could get an extra ID for her, and they could ride off into the sunset together.

She bit the inside of her cheek, trying hard not

to draw blood. What *would* she do once she got Max stabilized? He was a man who flew solo. He'd let her help him, and then he'd let her go. She could tell by the way he kept fighting his attraction to her.

And he *was* attracted to her, just as she was to him. All she could do right now was help. She owed him that.

"Drives like a dream." He tapped the steering wheel.

"A three-thousand-dollar dream with ninety thousand miles on it?" She rolled her eyes. "Let's just hope it can get us up to Salt Lake without incident."

He tapped the GPS that the dealer had thrown in with the deal. "Once we get the name and address of the resort where Cody's working, we can enter it and be on our way. Are you sure you don't want to use my phone to call him?"

"I'll wait until I get one of my own. Cody's not going anywhere. The ski season hasn't officially started yet."

He handed her the GPS. "Do you want to find the next midsize town? Someplace with a decent electronics store for the power cord? You can pick up a throwaway phone anywhere."

"Like I said, I'm in no hurry." She patted her gurgling tummy. "I'm more interested in finding some food."

"You should've had one of those bagels. How about a quick drive-through so we can get on the road?"

"Find me a breakfast burrito and I'll be happy."

"There are usually a few fast-food places around the freeway, so I'll keep going that way."

One block before the freeway on-ramp, Ava tapped the window. "That'll do."

Max pulled into the drive-through, ordered a burrito for her and a couple of coffees, and they were on the freeway five minutes later.

After Ava polished off her breakfast, she reached for the laptop in the backseat. "Do you think the battery's dead?"

"Not sure. What are you going to look for?"

She opened the computer and tried to power it on, but the battery had died. "I just wanted to check out the formula again. We should probably buy a thumb drive so we can copy the formula and print it out somewhere. If something happens to this computer, we'll be lost."

"Who knows? Tempest may even have a kill switch to Arnoff's laptop. If it leaves his possession, they may be able to shut it down remotely."

"They can do that?" Her fingers curled around the sides of the computer, her palms suddenly sweaty.

"Tempest employs top-notch people. You said it yourself—Dr. Arnoff was brilliant."

"He was. Too bad he used that brilliance for a terrible cause."

"He paid for it."

She rubbed the goose bumps on her arms. "As did everyone in the lab, whether they knew about the true purpose of T-101 or not."

"I'm sorry."

Turning her head toward the window, she blinked back tears. Max's sincerity ran deep. Maybe because he was in danger of losing his emotions, he relished them more than the average man.

There was no way she'd let him morph into Simon. She'd mix up a batch of that antidote if she had to hijack a hospital to do it.

A few hours later, they started seeing signs of civilization. Max pulled off the freeway, and they spotted an outdoor mall with several stores.

Max said, "We're in luck. We can get computer accessories in that electronics store on the corner."

"And find a place to work in one of the restaurants on the other side."

They bought a power cord that fit Dr. Arnoff's computer, a thumb drive and two temporary cell phones.

Ava nodded toward a coffeehouse at the edge of the mall. "If you're not too hungry, we can get a snack in there and plug in the laptop.

That's probably the only place with an outlet for us to use."

"That's okay with me."

They settled into a corner table next to a woman tapping away at her keyboard, and Max held up the plug. "Can I use the outlet beneath your table?"

The woman glanced up from her computer. "Sure."

Leaning back, Max plugged in Arnoff's laptop.

While Ava powered it up, he pointed to the counter. "Sandwich and coffee?"

"Just a latte for me."

The laptop woke up, and Ava dipped into the plastic bag on Max's chair and unwrapped the thumb drive. She inserted it into the USB port and navigated to the file containing the antidote formula. By the time she'd dragged the file to the external drive, Max had returned with her latte.

"They're microwaving my sandwich. Did you copy it over?"

"I did." She leaned back in her chair, wrapping her hands around the large coffee mug, inhaling the milky sweet aroma of her drink. "Now I can relax a little. You really had me on edge with that comment about a kill switch."

"Like I said—Tempest has experts in every

field." He tapped the back of the computer's cover. "Are you going to print it out, as well?"

"I think that's a good idea. Did you notice a copy place in this shopping center?"

"I didn't see one, but I'm sure we'll find a printer we can use in this town." He looked at his watch. "Now we just have eight hours until we get to Salt Lake. Are you going to call Cody now?"

"I'll turn on my cell long enough to copy his number from my contacts into this temporary phone and call him from the car when we can get some privacy." She scrolled through her contacts and punched Cody's number into the new phone.

The barista called from behind the counter. "Sir, your sandwich is ready."

As Max carried his sandwich back to the table, Ava pressed the button to turn off her cell phone and asked, "Who *is* behind Tempest, Max? Do you even know?"

"I know." His lips formed a firm line, and she raised her eyebrows.

"Does he have a name?"

"He has a code name—Caliban."

She snapped her fingers. "I get it. Caliban was the monstrous little character in *The Tempest*."

"Yeah, emphasis on *monstrous*." He picked up one-half of his sandwich and paused. "If I'd been more well-read, maybe I would've figured out the allusion. I didn't read that play in school. Then I found out the Caliban character tried to kill Prospero, and the code name suddenly made sense."

"Have you ever met Caliban?"

"No, but I know he's former military—special ops."

"Do you think someone turned him?" She blew on her coffee and took a sip.

"Someone or something, but he must've been off in the first place. You don't flip a switch like that and become a bad guy overnight. He definitely used his time in the military to make contacts. Tempest is a worldwide organization. It has no boundaries or loyalties—only to itself and its agenda."

"How do you know all this and the other agents don't?"

"I told you, Ava. The T-101 never worked right on me, or Simon. I don't know who else. I have to believe there are others. So, we suspected something was not right. I did some investigating while I was still in the fold. That's why I warned Simon to hang tough, but he couldn't do it."

"Does anyone else know anything about this? The CIA? Prospero?"

"God, I hope not." He broke his sandwich in half and prodded the crumbs on his plate with the tip of his finger. "The implications that the CIA or Prospero knows what Tempest is up to is too chilling to contemplate."

She narrowed her eyes. "But you've contemplated it."

"That's why I haven't contacted either agency. I'm not willing to take the risk." He took a bite of his sandwich and wiped his fingers on a napkin. Then he spun the laptop around to face him. "Have you checked the agent tracking program?"

"No. We're not going after anyone, Max. We need to work on this antidote. As it is, Cody is going to have to come up with the chemicals for the formula, even if he can find me a lab."

"We may not have far to go." He turned the laptop sideways on the table and flicked the screen. "It looks like this agent has come up from Mexico to Texas. It'll be easier to reach him now that he's in the States."

"After—" she closed the lid on the laptop "—we shoot you up with antidote."

"The sooner the better." He tapped her phone. "When you make that call to Cody, put him on Speaker."

"You don't trust me?"

"I don't trust him. Do you blame me?"

"Not at all." She popped the last bite of his sandwich in her mouth and dabbed her lips with a napkin. "In that case, I'd better make the call from the car. I don't want the cops coming down on me now as I discuss meth labs with my brother."

Max brought the plate and cups back to the counter and rapped his knuckles on the wood. "Is there someplace nearby where we can print a file from a thumb drive?"

"There's a twenty-four-hour copy shop about a mile down this street."

"Thanks."

When they got back to the car, Ava pulled the phone from her purse. "I'm not sure he's going to pick up a call from an unknown number."

"Leave a message."

She punched the speed-dial number for her brother and pressed the speaker button on the side. As she suspected, the phone rang four times and then voice mail picked up.

"Hey, man, I'm probably shredding. Leave me a message."

"Hi, Cody. It's me, Ava. Give me a call ASAP. I need a favor."

Max cocked an eyebrow. "Do you think telling him you need a favor is the best way to get him to call back?"

"*The* best way." She winked. "I told you he feels guilty about what happened before. I never ask him for favors, so he'll jump at the chance."

"Is he going to balk at the request?" He started

the car and maneuvered out of the shopping center's parking lot.

"Coming from me? Maybe. Coming from anyone else? Just another day in the life of Cody Whitman."

Max parked in front of the copy shop, and Ava patted the side pocket of her purse where she'd stashed the thumb drive. "Got it."

The clerk behind the counter directed them to a computer in the corner. "You can use that one. It'll scan your media first, and if there's a problem, you won't be able to continue."

Max waved. "I'm sure it's fine, thanks."

Ava inserted the thumb drive and printed out a copy of the file with the formula. When she took it off the printer, she folded it and stuffed it in her purse. "Okay, that's two backups."

On the way back to the car, her phone rang. "Cody?"

"Yep. What's up, Ava?"

"Hang on just a minute."

Max unlocked the car and they both slid inside. Then Ava put the phone on Speaker. "I need your help, Cody."

"I figured that from your message. Anything. You know I'm good for it."

Ava rolled her eyes at Max. "You're at Snow Haven, right? I'm on my way up to Salt Lake, and I need a lab."

"Yeah, yeah. Snow Haven." He coughed. "A lab? Aren't you still working for Dr. Arnoff?"

"It's a long story. I'll tell you later, but right now I need a place to work."

"I'd like to help you out, but how am I supposed to find you a lab?"

"Don't yank my chain, Cody. If you're not using, you know who is."

"Whoa, whoa. We are *not* discussing this over the phone."

"All right. We'll discuss it up there. I should be in town around ten o'clock tonight."

"Should I pick you up at the airport?"

"I'm driving in."

He whistled. "I don't even know what's going on with you right now, but I'm not sure I want to get involved."

"You don't have a choice, little bro." She looked at Max and shrugged. "Why are you so jumpy?"

"I didn't want to tell you, didn't want to worry you, but there's some weird stuff going on up here."

Ava's pulse picked up speed. "What are you talking about?"

"At work the other day, one of the other snowboard instructors told me someone was sniffing around looking for me—didn't sound like anyone I knew and he didn't give her a name."

"Maybe it was someone looking for lessons."

"I don't think so."

"Why are you so sure? You're in a tourist resort. It could be anyone asking about you."

"Two days later, I came home late from a party and someone had broken into my place and trashed it."

"What?"

"Yeah, and the weird thing is I think whoever trashed it was still there...waiting for me."

"What makes you say that?" Her hand gripped the small phone so tightly it almost popped out of her grasp.

"I just felt it, so I didn't go inside. Turned right around and headed for my buddy's place."

"Did you call the police?"

"I don't want to draw attention to myself here. My friend and I just went in and cleaned up later and then I got some new locks."

She blew out a breath. "Be careful, Cody. I'll call you when I get in tonight."

After she ended the call, Ava cupped the phone between two hands and twisted her head to the side to look at Max. "What do you think of all that?"

"I think Tempest tracked him down."

Chapter Eleven

Ava's eyes widened, but her grim mouth told him she'd already suspected the same.

"It makes sense. Tempest wouldn't have any trouble tracking down your brother, especially if he's already in the system." He closed his hand around hers to soften his words.

"I don't know about that, Max. I never put Cody's name on any paperwork. Dr. Arnoff knew about him, of course, but I didn't have him listed with HR. If they did track him down, d-do you think they'll hurt him?"

"They might…ah…try to get him to talk if they think he knows your whereabouts."

Her right eye twitched, and he smoothed his hand across her brow.

He said, "If they're watching him and he goes about his business, maybe they'll leave him alone."

"But not if he goes about his business finding me a lab."

He squeezed her hands. "Tempest is good but not that good, Ava. They still don't know how much we know, what we're after. They only know I've pieced together parts of their scheme and what they've been doing to the agents. They have no idea we're looking for a lab to mix up an antidote. They may not even know about the antidote."

"I'm pretty sure Dr. Arnoff didn't go blabbing to his superiors about testing the T-101 on himself, so maybe he never mentioned the antidote." Her fingers twisted beneath his hold. "I just don't want to drag Cody into this."

He got that. He hadn't wanted to drag Ava into this either, but Tempest had already done its part to make sure she was up to her neck in it. "We can turn around right now, find some other lab, abandon the whole project."

"No." She pinned her shoulders to the back of the seat. "This is your only chance, Max. We have to see it through."

"It's up to you."

"Snow Haven it is."

They crossed through a corner of Colorado, and the temperatures dropped as the elevation rose. Ava offered to drive, and they switched places.

They drove through another fast-food place for dinner, and Max vowed to wine and dine Ava once they got to Snow Haven. It sounded like a perfect place to relax and sink into luxury, but it wouldn't turn out to be much of a haven for them with Ava cooking up potions in a meth lab while they looked over their shoulders.

Maybe they'd both jumped to conclusions. Given Cody's lifestyle, it could've been anyone going through his stuff—maybe even the cops.

"We still have a few hours. You can take a nap if you like." She patted the GPS stuck to the windshield. "I can get there."

"We should've asked your brother for a hotel recommendation."

"Aren't we going straight to his place? I was going to call when we got to town to get his address."

"I don't want to go rushing up to his apartment, especially if it's been compromised. Let's get a feel for the place first."

"Cody's probably tending bar tonight anyway. I didn't even ask him."

He peeled the GPS from the glass and tapped it. "I think this will list hotels and restaurants, too. We can look something up when we get to Snow Haven."

"I wonder if they have any snow yet. Do you ski?"

"Yeah. Do you?"

"That's an expensive sport, and my family didn't exactly have money."

"How did Cody learn to snowboard?"

"Cody's been playing pretty much since he graduated from high school—snowboarding, surfing, mountain climbing. He's done it all."

"How'd he afford that lifestyle?"

"Don't ask." She pursed her lips and stared at the highway.

Max closed his eyes, but he'd never mastered the trick of sleeping in a moving car or plane or bus. He never got tired though. He was wound too tight to relax. Tempest must've thought he was prime material for their spy games.

"Are you okay to drive the rest of the way? I can't sleep anyway."

"I'm good." Her brow furrowed. "You need to get some rest."

"You mean because it's almost time for Mr. Hyde to come out?"

"I'm just wondering if you could hold out for a little longer if you practiced meditation or deep breathing or something like that."

He lifted his shoulders and let them drop. "Never tried it."

"My point exactly."

He slumped in his seat and closed his eyes again. "I'll start working on it right now."

A few seconds later, Ava was poking his arm. "We're here."

He blinked and rubbed the back of his stiff neck. "Where?"

"In Snow Haven, and it's not snowing."

"You're kidding." He pressed his forehead against the cold window, as the outline of stark trees rushed by in the dark. "I actually fell asleep."

She scrunched up her face. "It wasn't a very deep sleep—lots of mumbling and twitching."

"That must've been attractive. Any drooling?"

She giggled. "Not that I noticed."

He wiped his chin with the back of his hand anyway and dug the GPS out of the cup holder. He tapped the display for places of interest and selected hotels.

Several popped up and he scrolled through the list. "How about the Snow Haven Lodge and Resort."

"Sounds expensive."

"Tempest is footing the bill."

Her jaw dropped. "Is that where you got all this cash?"

"They owed me—big-time."

"Let's do it. It's not like you're going to return any leftover funds to Tempest, is it?"

"Not unless they pry them from my cold, dead hands."

Ava sucked in a breath and punched his shoulder. "Don't even joke about that."

Hadn't she figured out yet that he didn't have much of a sense of humor? He rubbed his arm. "Ouch."

"There's more where that came from if you insist on tempting the fates with that kind of talk."

Ava Whitman could be a fierce little thing.

He selected the Snow Haven Lodge and Resort, and the GPS told them to take the exit in two miles.

He yawned and shook his head. "I don't think I could take your brother tonight anyway. I need a good night's sleep, a meal and a shower first."

She tilted her head. "You don't think you could take Cody? I can't imagine you'd have anything to fear from him."

"Fear?" He snorted. "I'd be hard-pressed not to clock him for the way he treated you."

"Really?" Her voice squeaked.

"You've never had anyone look out for your interests?"

"I wouldn't say *never*. One of my professors in med school took me under her wing." She shook her hair back from her face. "Of course, she abandoned me when she discovered what I'd done."

"What Cody did. Didn't you ever tell her the truth?"

"I've never told anyone that truth, except Dr. Arnoff, who'd already heard the story from Cody. And you."

"Like I said, that brother of yours will be lucky if I don't knock his block off."

"Please, don't. We need his connections."

A little smile hovered around her lips as she took the exit, so he knew she kind of liked the idea of someone knocking her brother's block off for what he'd done to her.

A few miles in, Max pointed to an alpine structure set back from the road. "There it is. I'm hoping they have a vacancy since the season hasn't officially kicked off."

She pulled the tired little beat-up car up to the valet station and popped the trunk.

As she took the ticket from the valet, she asked, "Are there rooms available?"

"Yes, ma'am. We won't fill up for another month unless the snow comes early."

The bellhop pulled the duffel from the trunk first, staggering under its weight. Max made a grab for the strap and hoisted it over his shoulder. "I'll get this one. It has some sensitive equipment."

They approached the front desk with the bellhop wheeling the rest of their belongings behind them.

Max booked one of the suites. This way they'd

have two different rooms for sleeping without actually asking for two separate beds. He didn't know if he could handle another night lying next to Ava. He couldn't trust himself to keep his hands to himself.

The clerk slid two key cards toward them. "You're going to appreciate this suite. It has a fireplace and a wonderful view of the mountain."

Ava smiled brightly. "Perfect."

The bellhop trailed them to their room, and Max slipped him a tip after he'd unloaded their bags.

Ava wandered to the window and pulled back the drapes. "We could see the skiers from here if there were any."

"Are you hungry?" He shoved his bag in the closet.

"Not after driving all day and that icky fast food. Are you?"

"No, but I could use some water or a can of soda. Should we brave the minibar?"

"It's all courtesy of Tempest, right?"

He flung back the door beneath the flat-screen TV and opened the minibar. "Soda? Juice? Wine?"

"If you don't mind, I'll have some wine."

"Why should I mind?"

"I just figured you didn't drink. That's what you used to tell me during your checkups."

"I don't drink, but I don't mind if you do."

"We never recommended abstinence—from drinking. Did Tempest have some sort of rule against it? Not all of my agent patients were teetotalers."

"Red or white?" He held up two half bottles of wine.

"I'll take the red. It wasn't in the fridge, was it?"

"Next to it." He twisted off the lid and poured the ruby liquid into a glass. "My reasons for not imbibing aren't medical. I just never wanted to feel impaired in any way on the job."

"And you were always on the job, weren't you?" She strolled to him and took the wine-glass from his hand.

"Twenty-four seven."

"When's the last time you had a vacation?" She ran her fingertip along the rim of the glass before taking a sip.

"I can't even remember." He snapped the tab on his soda and gulped back the fizzy drink. "That was the point of the Tempest agents on T-101. We didn't need vacations. We're super-human."

She dropped to the love seat in front of the

fireplace and toed off her shoes. "I suppose I should call Cody and let him know we're here."

"Tell him we'll meet him for breakfast."

She put her phone on Speaker again and called her brother.

When he answered, he shouted across the line over raucous background noise. "Ava? What is this number, anyway? Not your usual."

"Never mind. I'm here at the Snow Haven Lodge and Resort. Do you want to come by here for breakfast tomorrow morning? Ten? I know you're not an early riser."

A shrill whistle pierced through the noise. "The Snow Haven Lodge and Resort? Dr. Arnoff must be paying you well."

"Can you get over here at ten?"

"I'll be there. Enjoy your fancy digs."

She pushed up from the love seat and plugged her phone into the charger. Then she placed her wineglass on the mantel and fiddled with the switch on the side of the fireplace.

"I think that ignites the pilot." He strode to the fireplace and picked up a box of long matches. "Turn it to the right, and I'll light the fire."

A little blue flame flickered beneath the logs and he struck a match and lit the kindling. The blaze raced along the log and then shot up into an orange fire.

"I like that." He grabbed his can and sat on

the floor before the fire, leaning against the love seat Ava had just vacated and resting his forearms on his bent knees.

She took a sip of her wine and gazed into the fire. "This feels good—almost normal."

"Have a seat." He patted the cushion behind him.

Cupping the bowl of her glass with one hand, she took a few steps toward the love seat and lowered herself to the edge.

The soft denim of the jeans encasing her legs brushed his arm. She stretched her feet out to the fire and wiggled her polished toes.

"How's the wine?"

"It's good. It's been a while since I've had a drink, too, except those few sips with Lillian Arnoff." She swirled the wine in her glass and took a gulp. "I can feel it sort of meandering through my veins, relaxing each muscle set as it warms it."

He twisted his head around to look at her. "Are you tipsy already?"

A slow smile curved her lips, which looked as red as the wine in her glass. "I don't think so, but I sure feel relaxed."

"Good. You've had a rough few days."

She sat forward suddenly, her hand dropping to his shoulder. "No, you've had a rough few days—a rough few months and maybe even a rough few years."

Tears gleamed in her green eyes. Maybe that wine hadn't been such a good idea after all.

He patted her hand. "I'm okay, Ava."

She slid off the love seat and joined him on the floor, stretching her legs out next to his. "What are you going to do once you get the antidote?"

"*If* I get the antidote, I'm going to try to reach out to the other agents. Tempest will have a tough time carrying out its plans without its mind-controlled agents doing the dirty work."

"Once we have the proof for the CIA or even Prospero, those agencies can take care of Tempest. You don't have to be a one-man show anymore." She yawned, and her head dropped to his shoulder.

"I'm not a one-man show." He snaked his arm around her shoulders. "I have you."

"Mmm." She snuggled against him. "Pill. Don't forget your pill."

Ava's breathing deepened, and Max let out a pent-up breath. Her exhaustion just saved him from battling his attraction to her. The suite, the view, the fireplace had all made him forget for just a minute who and what he was.

He disentangled his arm from Ava's shoulders. She stirred. He swept her up in his arms and carried her into the bedroom. He dipped and stripped back the covers on the bed with one hand. Then he placed her on the cool sheet and tucked the other sheet and the blanket around her chin.

She murmured, "Max?"

"Shh. Go to sleep."

He fished the breath-mint tin from his pocket and plucked out one of the blue pills. He swallowed the pill with the rest of his soda and then stretched out on the couch by the window.

He'd just protected himself and Ava from another one of his spells, but if Ava couldn't cook up that antidote he'd have to take more drastic measures to protect her.

He'd have to leave her.

AVA FLUNG HER arm out to the side, clutching a handful of sheet. Her lids flew open and she squinted against the light filtering through the drapes.

She ran her tongue along her teeth in her dry mouth. Had she gotten drunk and passed out? No wonder Max hadn't spent the night with her.

Max. A spiral of fear curled down her spine. Had he taken his pill last night or did he try to tough it out again?

She scrambled from the bed, still wearing the clothes from yesterday. "Max?"

She shot out of the bedroom and plowed right into his chest.

"Whoa." He grabbed her around the waist to steady her. "Are you okay?"

Brushing the hair from her face, she studied his clear, dark eyes and the smile hovering around his mouth. "I was worried about you."

He cocked his head. "Me? I'm not the one who went comatose after one glass of wine."

"I—I mean, I didn't know…"

"I took a pill before I went to sleep." He dropped his hands from her waist. "In fact, you reminded me right before you passed out."

She poked his hard stomach. "I didn't pass out. At least, I don't think I did."

"You were wiped out after that drive. Anyone would've fallen asleep after a glass of wine."

"At least it was one glass instead of the ten it took to put my mom under the table." She dropped her lashes. "You didn't have to sleep in the sitting room. I think we proved the other night that a king-size bed is big enough for the two of us."

His eyes flickered. "I didn't want to disturb you."

"No…incidents last night?"

"If you mean did I start gnashing my teeth and breaking out in a cold sweat, the answer is no. The pill worked just like it always does."

"Glad to hear it, but now you have just two left, so I need to get to work. Cody's meeting us at the restaurant at ten."

"No, he's not."

"Oh my God, did he call or something? Is he backing out?"

"I didn't talk to Cody, but I don't want him coming over here on his own. He might be followed. We still don't know who broke into his place and why or if they're still here."

"Should I have him meet us somewhere else?"

"Tell me where he is, and we'll pick him up so I can make sure he's not being tailed, and we can stop for breakfast somewhere else."

She ducked around Max and snatched her phone from the charger. "I'll call him right now."

When her brother answered the phone, he sounded half-asleep.

"Change of plans, Cody. My friend and I are going to pick you up. Is there someplace for breakfast around there?"

"Tons of places in the town of Snow Haven."

"Give me your address and wait outside for us. We'll be there at ten."

Cody rattled off his address and asked, "Who's your friend? Is she hot?"

"He is hot—very hot."

She ended the call and turned to face Max, who had looked up from his tablet. "I think you just disappointed Cody. Is he going to be a no-show now?"

"He'll be more curious than ever."

Forty-five minutes later, they were on the road to Cody's. Ava had shoved Dr. Arnoff's laptop into her bag and had the printed-out formula folded up and stuffed in her pocket. They'd put the thumb drive in the hotel safe, along with stacks of cash from Max's bag.

Max followed the directions from the GPS, and when they pulled onto Cody's street Ava tipped her chin toward her brother, dressed in jeans and a red flannel shirt, his hair scraggly. "That's him."

Max rolled the car to a stop at the curb, and Cody bent over and peered into the car. When he saw her, he broke into a smile, wreathed by a scruffy brown beard.

Max popped the locks on the car and Cody climbed into the backseat. "Hey, Ava, good to see ya."

"Cody, this is Max. Max, my brother, Cody."

Max looked into the rearview mirror and nodded.

"How you doing, man?" Cody settled against the backseat. "There's a breakfast place called Holly's about a half a mile up and to the left. So, what's this all about?"

"I'll tell you when we get to Holly's."

Assured they hadn't been followed from Cody's place, Max parked the car in a metered lot a half a block from the restaurant.

On the walk, Cody peppered her with questions about her job and Dr. Arnoff, which she avoided and deflected. Since Cody was a master of both, he didn't pressure her for answers.

They snagged a table in the back of the restaurant, near the kitchen. Cody and Max ordered full breakfasts with the works while she stuck with blueberry pancakes.

They traded comments about the weather and the drive and Cody's job until he planted his elbows on either side of his plate. "Are you going to tell me about this favor you want me to do, Ava?"

Max pointed his fork at Cody. "And don't forget, you owe her for destroying her career."

Cody's eyes bugged out. "You told him about all that, Ava? Are you crazy?"

"He had to know. It's all tied to what I need from you now."

"Spit it out."

"Are you still using, Cody?"

He glanced over his shoulder. "If by 'using' you mean addled, dazed and confused—no. I use a little for recreational purposes, mostly weed these days."

She sighed. "With our family background

and your own past addictions, I don't understand why you risk it."

"It is what it is, Ava." He shoveled more food into his mouth.

"Do you have a dealer in Snow Haven?"

As he wiped his mouth with his napkin, his murky green eyes narrowed. "Who wants to know?"

She shoved her plate away from her and her fork clattered to the table. "If I wanted to turn you in, I would've done so a long time ago."

Cody leveled a finger at Max. "You're not a cop, are you?"

"Do I look like a cop?" He glared at Cody's finger, and Cody dropped his hand.

"No, but you could be one of those undercover guys."

"I'm not. Look, we don't give a damn about your drug use, or at least I don't. We need a lab, and we need it yesterday."

Cody's brows disappeared under the messy curls across his forehead. "You mentioned a lab before. What is this all about, Ava?"

"I know you've been involved in the production of meth, Cody." She held up her hands. "Don't even bother lying to me."

"And you want me to secure a meth lab for you?"

"Exactly." She slid a piece of paper across

the table. "And it needs to be stocked with these chemicals."

He glanced at the list before pocketing it. "Why do you need all this?"

She folded her arms. "You have your secrets, and I have mine. You don't need to know. I need a place to work, and I need those specific chemicals."

"What about Dr. Arnoff? Don't you already have a lab where you work?"

"That lab is no longer feasible." Max took a sip from his coffee cup, watching Cody over the rim.

Cody balled up his napkin and tossed it onto his plate. "Are you in some kind of trouble, Ava? Is this guy taking advantage of you?"

Ava held her breath as her gaze darted to Max's clenched jaw.

"You have some nerve saying that after what you put her through."

Cody flinched. "I know I'm a jerk, but that doesn't mean I want my sister to get mixed up with anyone else who's going to hurt her."

Max's dark eyes got even darker. "I'm not going to hurt your sister."

Ava waved her hands between them. "Hey, I'm right here at the table. You don't have to talk about me like I'm not."

The waitress broke the tension with her coffeepot. "Refills?"

When the waitress left, Ava turned to Cody. "All you have to know is that Max and I are helping each other. I wouldn't be here right now without him."

"Okay, I believe you. So, I'm supposed to find you a lab, no questions asked."

"Last time I checked, cooking meth was illegal. We're the ones who won't ask any questions." Max wrapped his strong hands around his coffee cup.

Cody swallowed, his Adam's apple bobbing in his throat. "Deal. I have an option in mind, but just so you know, it won't be my lab and it won't come cheap. I don't cook the stuff."

"I don't care, but your sister does. For her sake, you should think about cleaning up your act."

Before Cody irritated Max any more, Ava tapped his water glass. "Tell me about the break-in. Was anything stolen?"

"Not that I could tell, but then, I don't have much stuff. I had my phone with me. I have a roommate and none of his stuff was taken either. The place was tossed. That's why I figured it might be the cops."

"The cops are going to break into your place

without a search warrant and go through your stuff?" Max shook his head. "I don't think so."

"You sure you're not a cop?"

"I'm sure, but I don't think the police operate that way."

Cody snorted. "You don't know the cops like I do."

"I'm sure nobody knows the cops like you do, Cody." Ava rolled her eyes. "How soon are you going to know about the lab?"

"Today." Cody scratched his beard. "He'll want to be paid. You good for that?"

"I am, but he'd better not try to gouge me." Max's voice had rolled into a growl.

"He won't, he won't. He's a good guy."

Ava made a noise in the back of her throat and her brother had the grace to turn red.

"I mean, for a guy who cooks meth."

Ava waved her hand in the air for the waitress. "Don't come to our hotel to see us. Give me a call on that number when you have something."

Max added, "And watch your back."

Cody's hand collided with his water glass. "Why do I need to watch my back?"

"Someone broke into your place, right?" Max lifted one shoulder. "I don't think it was the cops."

"Are you telling me that break-in had something to do with this lab business?"

Ava reached across the table and encircled Cody's wrist with her fingers. "Maybe. Just do me a favor and be careful."

"You too, Ava." He grabbed her hand. "You deserve to be happy. And safe—you've never been safe."

She slid a glance to Max tossing some bills on the check tray and whispered, "I'm safe now."

Max handed the money to the waitress. "Cody, can you get back to your place from here?"

"I get it. You don't want us to be seen together." He winked. "Done deal, man. Ava, I'll be in touch."

He leaned across the table and tugged her hair, and then he scooted out of the booth.

Max slumped in his seat. "He's a character. You two are nothing alike, except..."

"Except what?"

"Hard to explain." His hands formed a circlc. "A certain naiveté about the world, I guess."

"I'm not naive anymore, Max. I've seen too much."

"Sure you are, and that's part of your charm. You're able to hold on to the good even among waves of bad. It's a gift."

"You don't have to dress it up."

"I'm not." He tapped the table. "Let's get back to the hotel. I was looking at the spa services, and a massage sounds pretty good about now, doesn't it?"

"Sounds like heaven."

He opened the door for her and they stepped onto the sidewalk.

Max stopped in front of a kiosk and grabbed a local paper, perusing the front page while Ava scanned the notices pinned to the bulletin board.

Out of the corner of her eye, she noticed a man pivot suddenly and hunch forward to look in a shop window.

As she studied his profile, beneath the baseball cap pulled low over his forehead, her heart jumped. She grabbed Max's wrist. "I recognize that man to your left in front of the T-shirt shop."

Max didn't move a muscle, but his frame stiffened. "Who is he?"

"He's a Tempest agent."

Chapter Twelve

Max didn't turn around despite the adrenaline pumping through his veins—the adrenaline and the T-101, but that Tempest agent shopping for T-shirts would have even more T-101 pumping through his veins.

He dug into his pocket and pulled out some change and a pen. He shoved the coins in the slot for the paper and put his lips close to Ava's ear. "Take this pen. We're going to split up, so I can draw him away from you. If he comes after you and he gets close, flip off the lid to this pen and jab him. It's not ink… It's poison."

She sucked in a quick breath but she took the pen from him and curled her fingers around it. "What about you?"

He gave a slight nod to his right. "I'm going to lure him into that public restroom by the bus stop. I have my weapon."

"He'll have a weapon, too."

"He will." He nudged her hip. "Head down the

street like you're shopping. Go into one of those shops. He may follow you, but he's not going to shoot you down in broad daylight in the middle of a store."

"What if he has a knife or a poison pen of his own?"

"Like I said, Ava, if he gets close, stick him first."

Cupping her cheek with one hand, he kissed her mouth. "Goodbye, Ava."

He looked both ways before crossing the street, taking in the man with the baseball cap. He never would've known the guy was from Tempest.

When he reached the other side of the street, he glanced over to make sure Ava was on her way.

He window-shopped along the way to the bathroom, releasing a long sigh when the Tempest agent crossed the street to follow him. At least Ava was safe—for now. If he didn't come out of this encounter alive, she'd have the good sense to contact the CIA, or maybe she'd have the good sense to leave the country. Would Caliban want to leave any loose ends? He didn't think so.

The man was shortening the distance between them, but he wouldn't shoot him on the street, even with a silencer. The streets weren't crowded, but there were enough people to deter him.

He tensed his muscles and headed into the bathroom. The door had been taken off its hinges, but a divider wall separated the entrance from the urinals and stalls.

He slid his gun from his shoulder holster beneath his jacket and approached a urinal, turning to face the entrance.

The thought had crossed his mind that this agent might be someone like him and Simon. Even if he had the opportunity, could he just start shooting as soon as the guy walked in?

He didn't have to worry about that.

The agent emerged from behind the divider, his gun drawn.

Max immediately raised his own weapon. He recognized him now—the agent that was positioned in Central America on Arnoff's locator. So, he couldn't have been the same person who broke into Cody's apartment. He couldn't have made it here that quickly.

Snyder stretched his lips in what passed as a smile for a Tempest agent. "I should've known you'd be ready for me, Duvall. I'd considered tossing an explosive device in here, but that would've caused a scene. You know how much Caliban detests scenes."

"Yeah, he's a real low-key guy." He trained his

aim right between Snyder's eyes. "Looks like we have a standoff here."

"Not really. I don't care if I die for Tempest. You do. That gives me the upper hand. I start shooting, you start shooting, we both end up dead. And without you to protect her, Dr. Whitman will be next."

A quick, hot rage thumped through his system. He'd never allow that to happen. "Dr. Whitman already knows too much, and she'll know what to do once I'm gone."

"I don't think so."

"You're a drone, Snyder. Don't you care? You're a dispensable pawn to Tempest and your hero Caliban. You're drugged. You're a machine. I can help you."

"I don't want help. I've committed great acts of heroism for Tempest. We will rule the world one day."

"Is that what Caliban is after? He wants to rule the world?" Max tightened his finger on the trigger. Snyder had an automatic and would cut him down as he was getting his own shot off. But he *would* get the shot off.

"Caliban is a madman, like many before him. He'll never rule the world. He'll just succeed in murdering a lot of people and causing strife among countries."

"And that, Duvall, is the first step."

Snyder had lied. If he didn't care about dying, he would've pulled the trigger already.

"Come back to the fold, Duvall. You're too valuable an agent for Tempest to lose. Get back on the program. I know you have to be hurting right now. We can shoot you up with the juice and make it all better."

So that was Snyder's motive, to get him back to Tempest. If he pretended that was what he wanted, he could buy more time.

Max rubbed his temple. "It's hell coming down off the stuff."

Snyder's voice turned silky smooth. "You don't have to. The lab where Dr. Whitman worked, where we used to get our shots, has been destroyed. She destroyed it. She's our enemy now."

Was that the lie Tempest was spreading among its agents? It was designed to make Ava enemy number one, which would be laughable if it weren't life-and-death.

Max cleared his throat. "Where are we getting our shots now?"

Snyder hesitated, his eyes flickering. Tempest agents didn't do well when they had to make decisions like this on their own.

Straightening his spine, Snyder said, "Germany. We're going to Germany now, where the other testing takes place."

The other brainwashing, but Max was supposed to be a good little agent and not state the obvious.

"I don't know, man. It's hard."

"Come back, Duvall. We need you. The cause needs you."

Maybe if he went with Snyder, Tempest would forget about Ava, or he could convince them she knew nothing, was no threat.

"You'd take me to Germany now?"

"Yes. If I had orders to kill you, I would've done it before I walked into this bathroom."

He believed that. "And Dr. Whitman? We just leave Dr. Whitman? She really doesn't know anything. Hell, *I* don't know anything."

"Yes. We leave her here." Snyder shifted his gaze to the wall and back.

He was lying.

Max's muscles coiled. He'd take the shot and then die for it. Die for Ava. It would be the most human action he'd taken in a long time. He'd go out a man, not a machine.

His gaze focused on a point right between Snyder's eyebrows.

Max sensed a whisper behind the divider and then Ava emerged from behind it. In a flash, she lunged at Snyder and plunged the pen into the side of his neck. He dropped like a brick, his automatic weapon slipping from his hands.

It all happened so fast, Max still had his weapon pointing at thin air.

Ava grabbed a paper towel, wiped off the pen and tossed it in the trash. "Let's get out of here before the lunchtime bus service starts and someone actually comes into this bathroom."

"We can't leave him here with this weapon. The drug you just injected him with mimics a heart attack."

"Do your thing. I'll watch out for witnesses."

While Ava hovered near the door, he crouched beside Snyder's body and started breaking down his weapon. He threw some pieces into the trash can. The rest he'd toss into the Dumpster around the corner.

When he had the two longest pieces of Snyder's gun in his hands and his own weapon tucked back into its holster, he joined Ava at the door.

"Let's slip around the back. Do you see any cameras around here? I checked when I headed inside, but I didn't have much time."

They scanned the outside of the small dilapidated building and Max didn't detect anything. He grabbed Ava's hand and pulled her to the back of the bathroom. Then he leaned into the Dumpster and buried the two pieces of metal beneath a mountain of trash.

He wiped his hands on the thighs of his jeans.

"Let's do a little window-shopping on our way back to the car." He took her hand again and they strolled down the sidewalk like a couple of tourists, except Ava's skin had an unnatural pallor and her hand was shaking in his.

When they got to the car, she folded her frame in half and covered her face with her hands. Her shoulders shook and heaving sobs racked her body.

Although he wanted to take her in his arms, he wanted to get out of the area more, so he let her cry alone until he pulled the car into a turnout for a view point.

When he threw the car into Park and turned off the engine, he reached for her, running his hand along her back. "I'm sorry, Ava. I'm sorry you had to kill a man. You shouldn't have followed me, but you saved my life."

She rolled her head to the side, looking at him through wet lashes. "I don't care about killing him, Max. He was evil. I was just so afraid I wouldn't get there in time. And when I heard the last part of your conversation, when I heard him lie about letting me go, I knew you were going to shoot him. I knew you were going to die."

"Ava." He pulled her upper body across the console and she rested her head against his chest as he stroked her hair back from her moist face.

"I never expected you to come to my aid like

that. The pen was for your own protection. You shouldn't have put yourself in danger. Snyder would've been only too happy to shoot you dead if he'd seen you before you pulled that ninja move."

"I know, but I had to take the chance. You've taken so many chances for me."

He kissed the top of her head. "I appreciate it more than I can express. I'm just sorry it came to that. I never wanted to put you in a position like that."

She wiped her nose on his shirt. "Desperate times, desperate measures. Speaking of desperate, I need to check on Cody. He left the restaurant ahead of us. What if Snyder harmed him?"

"Call him."

She placed the call, holding the phone against her ear. "Yeah, yeah, I don't expect you to have anything yet. I'm just calling to see if you're okay."

She paused and nodded to Max. "Just checking. Everything's fine and we still need that lab and the chemicals."

She ended the call and dropped her phone in the cup holder. "He's okay. I didn't want to tell him what happened. He doesn't need to know any more than he already does."

"Do you think he'll suspect anything when he finds out a man died of a heart attack in the bus station bathroom minutes after we met for breakfast?"

"Cody pays very little attention to anything that doesn't involve Cody."

"Are you sure you're okay?" He threaded his fingers through hers.

"I'm fine. I'll be fine."

"Let's get back to the hotel, monitor the news and relax." He started the engine and pulled back into the stream of traffic.

"Maybe we can schedule those massages at the same time." Grabbing the back of her neck, she tilted her head from side to side as if to get the process started.

"I mentioned the massage for you, not me."

She jerked her head toward him. "Why not? You're the one Snyder was holding at gunpoint. You need it more than I do."

"I can't." He hunched his shoulders. "I don't really like massages."

Was there any good way to tell Ava that he didn't like to be touched? Except by her.

"I understand." She placed her hand on his thigh and he didn't even flinch under the gentle pressure.

He didn't need to explain. She got it. She got him.

He pulled in front of the hotel and left the car for the valet. As they walked into the lobby, he whispered in her ear. "I'm taking it as a good sign that there are no police here to greet us."

"Nobody saw what went down. That bus stop was deserted. I think it's mainly used during ski season as a shuttle stop and at lunchtime."

They got into the elevator with another couple, and Ava stopped talking. As soon as the couple got off, she turned to him as if she'd never stopped. "There weren't any cameras there either. What are the police going to find when they check his ID?"

"A man who has a convenient next of kin only too happy to take care of all the details."

When the elevator reached their floor, she straddled the doors holding them open. "Do *you* have convenient next of kin?"

"Absolutely."

"What about Simon Skinner? He had a fiancée—Nina. He talked about her all the time."

He corrected her. "He *had* a fiancée. They'd split up. She left him."

"So, Tempest won't even notify her?"

"No, but I wanted to notify her. It doesn't seem right. She'll never know what happened to Simon."

"It doesn't, but don't you think Tempest is going to be monitoring her now? They might suspect that you'll contact her."

He unlocked the door to their suite and pushed it open. "You're probably right."

"Like I said before, you need to worry about yourself right now. Look at Snyder. You were all ready to rush off to warn him and he was on his way to capture or kill you." She swayed on her feet and he caught her around the waist.

"You're not fine, Ava. You just killed a man."

"I-it was self-defense." A tremble rolled through her slight frame.

"And totally justified. I know that, but it doesn't make it any easier. Even if you took him out while he was pointing a gun right at your head, you'd still feel traumatized. Anyone with any human emotions would feel the same way. That's why Tempest had Dr. Arnoff create T-101—to develop agents without those human emotions. Killing machines."

She looked into his eyes. "That's not you. They couldn't do it to you."

"I've done my share…"

"Shh." She placed two fingers against his lips. "That wasn't you, and then you fought it. You're still fighting it…and you're going to win."

He kissed her fingertips. "Only with your help."

"It's the least I can do after you saved me from Simon and then those two assassins at my house, even after I'd been responsible for your predicament."

"I thought we were over the blame game. You didn't know what you were doing."

"And neither did you when you were working for Tempest."

"Then we're both guilt-free and can move on." He stuck out his hand. "Agreed?"

"Agreed." She shook his hand, and he rubbed his thumb across her smooth skin.

"I meant it about that massage. You look all wound up."

"And what are you going to do while I'm getting pampered?"

"Work." He walked to Dr. Arnoff's laptop on the desk by the window and turned it on. "I'm curious if that agent-locator program shows Snyder here in Snow Haven."

"That would be one way to make sure it's accurate. You're off that grid, so we can't check the accuracy that way."

Max drew his eyebrows over his nose. "So, how did Snyder find me? How'd he know to head to Snow Haven, Utah?"

Ava stopped digging through her suitcase and looked up. "I thought we determined that they'd tracked us down through Cody."

"Maybe someone on Tempest's orders initiated the break-in at Cody's place, but that was no Tempest agent or he would've shown up on the locator."

"Tempest found Cody and sent an agent here to follow up. He didn't show up on the locator because he wasn't here yet."

"The agent knew we were here one day after we arrived. How'd they get that info from Cody's apartment? They couldn't have."

"You said you got rid of your cell phone. That's how they'd been tracking you before. They must've just gotten lucky this time."

"Yeah, lucky." He navigated to the agent-locator program and pulled up the map. "Son of a... Ava, look at this."

She stood rooted to the floor, clutching a T-shirt to her chest. "I'm almost afraid to see."

"You're the kind of woman who wants to know what you're up against, right?" He didn't want to heap any more bad news onto her already fragile psyche, but they were partners in this thing and he needed her up to speed.

She squared her shoulders and joined him at the desk. "What are we looking at?"

"The locator map." He jabbed his finger at the display. "It shows Snyder here in Utah."

"Okay, so we know it works. That's a good thing, right?"

"Look at the other dots." He trailed his finger

across the map from east to west. "You notice anything about the location of these agents?"

"One's on the West Coast and one's on the East Coast. So what?"

"Yesterday, this one was in Southeast Asia and this one was in France. They're converging on us, Ava."

Chapter Thirteen

His words sucked the air from her lungs and she grabbed for the desk with one hand. "Snyder must've told them we were here."

"Impossible." He exited the program. "These agents were already on their way before Snyder even made contact with us. Tempest always knew we were headed to Snow Haven."

She licked her lips. "How? How could they be so sure just because Cody was here? Tempest can't possibly know what we have planned and how Cody can help us. Caliban may not even be aware of the antidote."

Max shoved the laptop and then landed his fist on the desk beside it. "It's the laptop. It's reciprocal. While the program tracks the agents, Tempest can track Dr. Arnoff. They found us at Arnoff's house. They knew Arnoff was dead, and they killed his wife. Once the laptop went on the move, they had to know it was us."

She stepped back from the desk on wobbly

legs. "We thought it was such a great find at the time, and it ended up betraying us."

"It's not human, Ava, and it *was* a great find. You discovered the formula for the T-101 antidote. Now you have the antidote printed out and on a thumb drive. It's time to get rid of the laptop."

"If we just destroy it, they'll have no reason to believe we left Utah."

"Exactly, which is why we have to do something other than destroy it."

"Which is?"

"Send it on a trip."

"How are we going to do that?" She clutched her hands in front of her. Everything was moving too fast.

"Think about it." He tapped his temple. "We're in a tourist area, in an upscale resort. People are flying in and out of Snow Haven all the time."

"Are you crazy?" She took a turn around the room, scooping a hand through her hair. "Nobody is going to take a laptop from us. TSA agents even warn people against it at the airports."

"Did I say we were going to ask?" He spread his hands. "I'm going to get into the hotel luggage area and slip it into someone's bag, after deleting everything on it except the locator program, which won't make sense to anyone else anyway."

"How are we going to do that?"

"There's no *we* this time. You go off and get your massage, and I'll get rid of the laptop." He strode toward her, cupped the side of her head in his large hand and smoothed a thumb between her eyebrows. "Don't worry about it. This sort of thing is a piece of cake for me. This laptop will be on its way to Boston or Atlanta or San Diego in no time, and those agents will have to adjust their travel plans."

To forget about everything for an hour or two and leave this in Max's capable hands sounded too good to pass up. Besides, those Tempest agents were still thousands of miles away, weren't they?

She took a deep breath and blew it out, ruffling the edges of his long hair. "Okay, but what if you get caught?"

He folded his arms and raised one eyebrow. "Really?"

"Okay, okay, piece of cake."

"Get on the phone and see if you can get an appointment right now. I'll start deleting stuff from the laptop."

The spa had an available appointment for a full body massage in twenty minutes and she took it.

She peered over Max's shoulder as he dragged files into the trash can and then emptied the trash. "It's a ninety-minute massage. Will the deed be done by then?"

"Yep. You just relax and enjoy, knowing we're sending those Tempest agents on a wild-goose chase."

"Not sure I'll be able to relax."

"Sure you will. I've got this, Ava."

She believed him. She trusted him. He'd been ready to take a bullet for her in that bathroom or even return to Tempest. She'd had to prove that he hadn't misplaced his trust even though sticking that man—Malcolm Snyder—in the neck with the pen had been just about the most frightening action she'd ever taken. She'd had to stuff down every memory of Snyder, every feeling she'd ever had about him, and go on autopilot.

That was how the T-101 worked. It put those agents on autopilot to allow them to do their jobs without question.

She shivered and pulled on a clean T-shirt. She didn't blame Max one bit for wanting off the stuff.

"I'm going to head down to the spa now. Should I just meet you back up here?"

"Hang on." He clicked the mouse without looking up. "I'm going to walk you there."

She wrinkled her nose. "I thought you said

we were safe for now, no Tempest agents in the immediate vicinity."

He dragged one more file to the trash can and looked up with a half smile on his face. "I just want to walk you down."

"I thought you wanted to let me in on the whole truth and nothing but the truth?"

He shoved a card key in his back pocket and placed his hand on her lower back. "I think we're safe right now, but nothing is one hundred percent."

"Okay, I can accept that."

They took the elevator down to the basement floor, one level below the lobby, and Max walked her to the door of the spa. He touched his lips to hers. "Enjoy yourself."

Ava checked in, relaxed in the waiting room with a cup of tea and some aromatherapy and then followed her masseuse to one of the back rooms. When the masseuse left her, she undressed and slipped beneath the sheet on the table.

She closed her eyes, the hushed atmosphere of the spa already working its magic and the gentle New Age music soothing her nerves. What if she told the masseuse that she'd just killed a man in a bus station bathroom? The Hippocratic oath she'd taken never seemed further out of reach.

The masseuse returned to the room, and they

exchanged very few words as she started working on her back.

The masseuse cooed. "You have a lot of tension in your shoulders and neck. I'm going to work on those knots."

Lady, you have no idea.

Ava responded with an unintelligible murmur as the masseuse dug her thumbs into her flesh.

Ninety minutes later, kneaded, pinched and pounded, Ava rose from the table a new woman. She paid with Tempest's cash and left a generous tip.

Back in the real world, she hoped Max had gotten rid of that laptop without getting detained by hotel security. She hoped someone had discovered Snyder in the bathroom and had already ruled his death a heart attack. And she hoped her brother had come through with a usable lab and the chemicals she'd need to mix up a batch of T-101 antidote. Was that asking too much?

She could feel the tension creeping back into her shoulders already. Maybe the spa could give her a daily appointment—she'd need it.

Stepping from the spa, she spotted Max lounging against the wall down the hallway past the gym. The stress that had been clawing its way back into her muscles melted away.

Maybe she just needed a daily appointment with Max.

When she approached, he pushed off the wall. "I don't even have to ask how it was. You look… relaxed."

"I'll be more relaxed once you tell me how things went on your end." Despite herself, she scooped in a breath and held it.

"Arnoff's laptop is safely on its way to Florida."

"Where it will get plenty of fun in the sun." She touched his arm. "Do you think it'll work?"

"It bought us a little time, although we don't know who's here checking up on your brother."

"Maybe that was a simple break-in. God knows, Cody attracts his share of trouble without even trying."

"I doubt it, but at least we know the person here working for Tempest is not one of the T-101 agents. They're all being tracked with that program. I might have some trouble handling another T-101 robot, but not anyone else."

"That massage made me incredibly hungry. Did you eat lunch yet?"

They continued past the gym and he pointed at the weight machines behind the glass. "I could use some lunch, and then I'm going to work out. If I can't take advantage of the spa here, I'm going to at least use the gym."

"Sandwiches in the lobby restaurant?"

He took her arm and propelled her down the hallway. "If you don't think you'll float away."

She covered a yawn with her hand. "Do I look like I'm floating?"

"Yep, and I'm glad to see it. I told you I'd take care of the computer."

She pressed the elevator button. "What about Snyder?"

"It just so happens that I overheard a couple of the bellhops talking about a man found in the men's room at the bus stop—an apparent heart attack victim."

She held up her crossed fingers. "Let's hope the coroner concurs with the initial finding."

"Believe me, Snyder's next of kin will make sure that they relate a history of heart disease. Tempest protects and conceals the deaths of its agents. You haven't heard anything about what happened in New Mexico, have you?"

"Not a word."

They sat down at the restaurant and she ordered a salad while Max stuck with a French dip sandwich. Just as she was about to dig into her salad, her cell phone buzzed in her pocket.

She pulled it out and smiled. "It's Cody. He says he's working on it."

"That's vague, but I'll take it."

"That's a lot from Cody. He's really trying to communicate."

"Let's hope he can nail this down for us."

She crunched through her vegetables to avoid the question on her lips. What would happen if Cody couldn't find them a lab? The formula and instructions for the antidote wouldn't do her any good without the chemicals to cook it and a lab to cook it in.

Since Max had taken a huge bite of his sandwich, she had to assume he didn't want to discuss it either.

He had two blue pills left, and he had to take one tonight. That didn't leave them a lot of time until…

She grabbed her soda and slurped through the straw. "If you don't mind, I'm going to let you hit the gym on your own. I'm going to take a nap. That massage made me feel like a limp noodle."

"That's okay. I'm not a very social gym rat. I'd rather listen to music than talk."

She traced a bead of moisture on the outside of her glass. "I suppose talking's a girl thing, huh?"

He crossed one finger over the other and held them in front of his face. "My mother taught me never to stereotype girls."

"Smart woman, your mom."

"Yeah. Smart and a little bit reckless." He clinked his glass with hers. "Like someone else I know."

"I'm not reckless. I just always end up in the wrong place at the wrong time."

"Like in the men's room at the bus stop with a poison pen clutched in your hand."

"Okay, maybe a little reckless."

Max paid the bill and Ava took a soda to go. When they returned to the room, Max retreated to the bathroom and changed into some basketball shorts and a tank.

"Just to be on the safe side, when I'm gone lock the dead bolt and don't answer the door. I'm not going to send you room service or a special note or anything else. If it's the housekeeping staff, it can wait. Okay?"

"Okay, but your words keep belying your assertion that we're safe."

"Ava." He sat next to her on the bed. "We're not going to be safe until this is over. You know that, right?"

She dipped her chin to her chest. "I do, but sometimes I just need to hang on to the illusion. Do you know what I mean?"

He curled a lock of her hair around his finger. "I know exactly what you mean. We can pretend everything's normal once in a while."

She parted her lips because she really, really wanted him to kiss her—and not one of those soft, gentle kisses he'd been bestowing on her as if she'd crack beneath any pressure from his lips. She wanted a real kiss—a hot, full-bodied, gasping-for-air kind of kiss.

He released her hair and stood up, reaching for his tablet on the bedside table. "You're welcome to go through my library and read something if that'll help you fall asleep."

"I'm not sure I'll need help. I'm pretty exhausted."

"You have reason to be." He peeled his card key from the credenza and pointed it at her. "Lock the dead bolt behind me."

She bounded from the bed when he closed the door, knowing he'd be waiting to hear the dead bolt. After she flicked it into place, she smiled as she heard his footsteps retreat down the hallway.

So, no hot kiss. Maybe she wouldn't get one until this was all over. He'd get so carried away when she shot him up with the antidote, he'd crush her into his strong arms and kiss her silly.

She snorted. She'd better hang on to that daydream because that was all it was. And did she really want a gratitude kiss?

She grabbed his tablet and fluffed a pillow behind her. Actually, she'd take anything he had to offer, motivated by anything.

She clicked the tablet, and his current book popped up. She scanned the text—one of Homer's epic poems. Didn't he say he wasn't well-read? Maybe after missing the Caliban reference, he decided to get well-read—or he was using this as a sleep aid.

She clicked back to the book list and noted some history, some true crime and a fantasy series. Max Duvall would probably never cease to surprise her.

She started in on the fantasy because she needed a little escape from this world. After reading about ten pages, she realized the fantasy world was no better than the real world— at least her real world.

She clicked the remote for the TV and crossed her legs at the ankles, tapping her feet together. She stopped the channel surfing at a reality dating show. Now, *this* was a fantasy she could get into.

By the time the show ended, Max was at the door. She peeked through the peephole and flipped back the dead bolt. "Wow, did you lift every weight in there?"

He pushed a damp lock of hair from his eyes, and his biceps bulged. "Yeah, sorry. I need a shower. Any news from Cody?"

"Nothing yet, but I think that woman should choose the dog trainer for the next date."

His brows shot up. "What?"

She flicked her fingers at the TV. "I got very engrossed in that show. Now I'm going to have to follow it and see who she picks."

"I thought you were supposed to take a nap."

She muted the TV. "I didn't feel that tired, but honestly vegging in front of the TV is pretty relaxing."

"Don't do much of that?"

"Not usually." She ran her gaze up and down his body, trying not to get hung up on a particular part of it. "How was the gym?"

"Good. I've lost some strength."

"That's good?" She covered her mouth. "Oh, the T-101 is having less of an effect on your body."

"Seems like it." He jerked his thumb over his shoulder. "I'm going to take a shower. You can indulge in more reality TV if you like."

"Funny thing about reality TV."

He cranked his head over his shoulder when he got to the door of the bathroom. "What's that?"

"It's so much more fake than real life, I don't know why they call it reality TV."

"Probably to make it seem like your own life is incredibly boring."

"Those reality TV people don't know my life."

"Right." He shut the door behind him.

She skimmed through the rest of the channels and left the TV on the local news. Maybe there would be some more information about Snyder. She hoped by the time his so-called next of kin came to Snow Haven to pick up the body, Tempest would be tracking them to Florida.

Max emerged from the bathroom with a towel

around his waist. "I forgot to bring some clean clothes in with me."

She'd seen it all before, but the first time she'd seen him half-naked she still thought he was a crazy person. Now he was everything to her.

She clamped her hands over her waist, stilling the butterflies. She didn't want to feel that way. Red flags and danger signs were waving and flashing in front of her eyes.

He stopped on his way to his bag and turned. "Are you okay, Ava?"

"Yeah, I'm fine."

He crossed the room and put the back of his hand against her forehead. "You looked pale. The whole incident in the bathroom rattled you more than you probably even realize. You could even experience some post-traumatic stress."

She'd been more upset about her unrequited feelings for Max than about killing a man. What did that say about her? She'd never admit that to Max.

"I'm just anxious."

He stroked her hair. "Understandable."

Her phone rang and she jumped to grab it from the nightstand. When she saw Cody's name on the display, she punched the speaker button.

"What do you have for us, Cody?"

"Nothing. I got nothing for you, Ava. There is no lab."

Chapter Fourteen

Her legs turned to rubber and she sank to the bed. "What are you talking about? You know people. There has to be someone in the area cooking meth."

"I'm not getting any hits, Ava. I'm sorry." He cleared his throat. "On the plus side, I got the other stuff you needed."

"What am I supposed to do, Cody, cook it up in the hotel bathroom?"

"I don't know what to tell you. The only possibility I have is out of town. He'll be back next week. I can probably set you up then."

She gripped the phone with two hands. "We don't have until next week. We don't have two days."

"I'll keep working on it, Ava. Maybe something will come through. These guys are cagey."

"Obviously. That's why we gave you all that money." Tears had filled her eyes and she dashed them away. "You owe me, Cody. You ruined my life, my career. I protected you, and now you owe me."

"I know that. I'll keep looking, Ava."

When she ended the call, she chucked the phone across the room and fell back on the bed, the tears running into her ears.

Max had stood silent and still like a statue during her conversation with Cody. Now the mattress dipped as he sat down beside her.

He wiped away her tears with the back of his hand. "It's okay, Ava. Don't cry."

She hoisted herself up on her elbows. "How can you say that? You know what it means, Max. You have two pills left—one for tonight and one for tomorrow. After that, you're cut off."

"Maybe I'll find more. That's where I was when I met up with you. I had no hope for an antidote then. I'm back to my original position."

"No, you're not." She tossed her hair back from her face. "You had five pills when you rescued me from Simon."

"If I had never gone to that lab to chase after Simon, I'd still have two pills today—and you'd be dead." He lay down next to her and captured her hand. "I'd say I'm in a lot better position now."

She sniffled. "What will you do, Max? How can I help you?"

One corner of his mouth lifted and he kissed

her fingers. "You've already helped me, Ava. Nothing more is necessary. Nothing more is required. We have a new goal now—get you to a secure location."

"Max." She twined her arms around his neck and pulled his head close to hers, pressing her forehead against his. "I don't want to lose you. Stay with me. I'll help you ride it out."

He wrapped one arm around her waist, and his other hand skimmed up her spine and cupped the back of her head.

Slanting his mouth across hers, he whispered her name against her lips.

The towel had come loose from his waist, and she trailed her hand down the warm, smooth skin of his back. Her fingers dug into the hard muscle of his buttocks, and she moved in closer to him, drawing him closer to her.

He deepened the kiss, thrusting his tongue inside her mouth, lighting a fire in her belly, curling her toes. Here it was at last—the hot kiss she'd longed for, but now it meant goodbye.

He yanked off his towel and tossed it over his shoulder onto the floor.

Her eyes still closed, she let her hands create the visual as they roamed over his naked body, skimming the hard muscle and the flat planes, caressing the smooth skin.

He ended the kiss, leaving her panting and

disoriented. Her lashes fluttered and her gaze met his dark eyes, alight with passion and desire. The look from those eyes melted her core.

Then she drank in what her hands had been exploring, and the beauty of his form took her breath away. Pure muscle cut through his lean frame. The nicks and scars on his body relieved it of perfection but added a layer of sexiness and danger that fueled her attraction.

On impulse, she ducked her head and planted her lips against the chiseled slabs of muscle on his chest. Her tongue toyed with one brown nipple, and she felt his erection plow into her belly.

With one hand, she reached down between his thighs and encircled his hard, tight flesh with her fingers.

A groan escaped his lips as he thrust into her hand. His fingers curled around the hem of her T-shirt. "Why are you still dressed?"

Before she could form a coherent answer, he had tugged the shirt from her body and over her head. It joined the towel on the floor. He slipped one hand into the cup of her bra, kneading her breast, swollen and aching with want.

His thumb trailed across her nipple, and she sucked her lower lip between her teeth to keep from screaming. He unclasped her bra and cupped both of her breasts in his hands. Dip-ping his head, he encircled one nipple with his tongue and then sucked it into his mouth.

"Oh." She dragged her fingers through his thick hair, her nails digging into his scalp. She hitched her leg over his hip to get even closer to him, and the head of his erection skimmed her bare belly.

She needed more of that.

She struggled with the buttons of her jeans with trembling fingers until Max drew back from her.

"Need some help with that?"

"If it means you have to stop doing what you were doing to my left breast, I think I got this."

He chuckled and unbuttoned her fly with deft fingers. "I have plenty of time to return to that luscious left breast."

At the mention of time, her heart jumped and she yanked off her jeans and her panties in one stroke. They had precious little of that and she intended to make every second count.

She kicked her pants to the floor and rolled onto her side again where Max awaited her. Wrapping his arms around her, he pulled her body against his. They met along every line, bare skin touching bare skin, fusing together in heat and passion.

With their arms entwined around each other, Max bent his head and captured her lips again.

She invited him inside, their tongues dueling and exploring.

His heart beat against her chest, strong and steady while hers galloped and skipped. She stroked him from his broad shoulders to the curve of his buttocks, reveling in the raw power tingling beneath her fingers.

He cupped her derriere with one hand, the calluses on his palm tickling her tender skin. He caressed her flesh and fit her pelvis to his as his erection prodded her impatiently.

When he broke away from her, he planted a path of kisses from her chin, down her throat and between her breasts. Then he cinched her around the waist and rolled her onto her back.

Missing the contact already, she reached for him, dragging her nails lightly across his six-pack.

He shivered, and then rising to his knees, he positioned himself between her legs, his body proud and masculine on display before her. If just the sight of him turned her to jelly, how would she be able to hold herself together once he entered her?

She'd have to wait to find out, since Max had other ideas.

Slipping his hands beneath her bottom, he lifted her hips. He leaned forward, kissed each breast, flicked his tongue down her belly and nibbled the soft flesh of her inner thighs.

She thrashed her head from side to side. "You're going to drive me crazy."

He rested his head against her leg, his hair tickling her. "Do you know how long I've waited to drive you crazy like this?"

She rolled her eyes toward the ceiling. "Ever since I saved your life in the bathroom?"

"Nope, before that." His tongue darted from his mouth, flicking against the sensitive skin between her legs.

She sucked in a sharp breath. "Ever since I saved your life at the Desert Sun Motel?"

"Before that." He teased her again with his tongue.

She squirmed, her hips bouncing from the bed. "Ever since I saved your life that first night in Albuquerque?"

He raised his brows. "Do you think this is gratitude I feel for you right now?"

"Mmm, this feels a lot better than gratitude."

"I'm glad you recognize that." He trailed his tongue up the inside of her thigh and brushed it across her throbbing outer lips.

She closed her eyes and let out a long sigh, even though her muscles had coiled in anticipation of a sweet release. "So, how long have you been waiting to drive me crazy?"

"Ever since you first had me strip to my skivvies in your examination room."

Her lids flew open. "Really?"

"Oh, yeah. You couldn't tell by my—" he coughed "—reaction to you?"

She giggled, the heat rising to her cheeks. "I thought your heart rate was a little elevated."

He snorted. "It wasn't my heart rate that was elevated, sweetheart. Now it's payback."

He ran his thumb along the outside of her moist flesh and then used his tongue and lips to drive her crazy.

All at once, everything came unraveled and she cried out as her orgasm jolted through her body. This was no smooth wave of pleasure. Instead her ecstasy clawed at her over and over, driving her to new heights. Max rode it out with her, shoving his fingers inside her, prolonging her release as she tightened around him.

When she lay spent, her breathing ragged and her chest heaving, he straddled her. Was the T-101 responsible for that erection? If so, she gave a silent, guilty thanks to Dr. Arnoff.

And then the guilt and the fear and the desperation all dissipated like feathers in a strong gust of wind as Max thrust into her. She closed around his thick girth as if he was a part of her.

He was a part of her. Whatever happened to him, to them, he'd always exist deep in her pores.

Each time he pulled out, even though it was for a nanosecond, she ached for his return. He plowed into her, over and over, as if he couldn't get enough, couldn't get close enough.

Her sensitive flesh, still tingling from her orgasm, responded to the close contact of Max's body, the tension building in her muscles again. She clawed at his buttocks, wanting more of him, needing more of him.

When he paused to capture her lips with his own, she shattered beneath him, her orgasm sending rivers of tingles throughout her body. She thrust her hips forward to engulf him and the motion acted like a trigger.

His frame stiffened as he plunged deep into her core. Then he howled like a wild, untamed beast and she trembled beneath him.

His release racked his body until sweat dripped from the ends of his hair, and his legs, still straddling her, trembled. He held himself above her, wedging his arms on either side of her shoulders. Then he lowered himself and kissed her mouth.

He growled. "I could do that all over again."

She dabbed her tongue against his salty shoulder. "Is that the T-101 talking?"

Grinning, he pulled out and rolled to her side. "Is that why you instructed your brother to fail on the lab?"

"Max." She drew her brows over her nose, and he tweaked it.

"I'm just kidding. You have to excuse my sense of humor. It's been AWOL for a few years." He smoothed the back of his hand across her cheek. "Let's just enjoy the time we have left."

Blinking back the sudden tears that flooded her eyes, she shifted to her side and smoothed her hand along the hard line of his hip. "I can do that."

"Glad to hear it." He rolled onto his back and pulled her close, molding her against his side. "You think we can find that reality dating show again?"

She twisted around and felt for the remote control on the bedside table. "Not sure about that show, but I'm sure we can find something that has more drama than our lives."

She aimed the remote at the TV and clicked the power button.

The hotel phone on the nightstand jangled and the hand Max had been circling on her belly froze.

They both stared at the phone as it rang again.

Ava swallowed. "I-it could just be housekeeping."

"Don't answer it."

They watched the phone ring three more times, Ava holding her breath until it stopped.

Max's entire demeanor had shifted from the passionate, considerate lover to the wound-up spy on the run, his jaw tight and his fists curled. She wanted to smash the phone with her own fist.

"Maybe we should call the front desk and see if it was housekeeping."

Max leveled a finger at the phone. "Whoever it was left a message."

She jerked her head to the side and eyed the blinking red light on the phone with trepidation. "That's good. Maybe they just want to drop off towels."

Max sat up and reached across her. He pulled the phone onto the bed. He punched the message and the speaker buttons in succession.

The automated voice droned. "You have one new message. To listen, press two."

He punched the two button. A rasping breath burst over the line, followed by a man's harsh voice. "Max, it's Adrian Bessler. I'm a Tempest agent and I need help."

Chapter Fifteen

Max put his finger to his lips as Ava started talking, her voice rising with each word.

The agent—Bessler—coughed and cleared his throat. "This isn't a trap, I swear. I know what happened to Skinner. I know what's happening to you. It's happening to me, too. We can help each other. I'll tell you more, but you have to meet me. I'm afraid to talk on this phone. I'll keep it for a while longer to wait for your call, and then I'm throwing it away. Hurry." He recited his phone number and then the message ended.

Max stared at the phone in his hands. "It's too convenient."

"I know Adrian Bessler, Max, and he didn't show up on the agent-locator program. I never thought to count those red dots on the map to verify if all the agents were accounted for, but I know Bessler's name wasn't among them."

"That doesn't mean anything." He slammed

the phone in its cradle and Ava jumped. He closed his eyes. "I'm sorry."

"It's okay." She rubbed the back of his hand with her fingers. "I realize it all could be a ruse, but he wasn't on that map."

"That could all be by design. Maybe Tempest figured since you were with me and had treated all the agents that you would've noticed Bessler's absence on the map, making this call more believable."

"But what if it's the truth?" She curled her fingers around his hand and squeezed. "You said yourself that you wanted to track down the other agents and warn them. Now you don't have to. One has come to you."

He pinched the bridge of his nose, squeezing his eyes closed. "I'd have to be very careful meeting him."

"Of course, and I'll be there, too."

"Forget it."

She squeezed his hand tighter. "I thought we were partners. I, at least, will know what Adrian Bessler looks like. That'll give us an advantage. You'll be walking in blind. He could be anyone—and that's dangerous."

"You could describe him to me. I'll tell him to wear something specific for the meeting."

She opened her eyes wide. "Didn't I ever tell you I'm really bad at describing other people?

Besides, he could tell you he'll be wearing a red baseball cap and then blindside you. With me, there will be no blindsiding."

He shoved the phone to the foot of the bed and took Ava into his arms again. Her silky, soft skin soothed him. "I don't want you in harm's way, my love."

She sipped in a small, quick breath and he mentally gave himself a good swift kick. He hadn't meant to mention anything about love, but after the incredible connection they'd just shared, the words had come to his lips naturally.

"If you don't want me in harm's way, then don't leave me—ever." She nuzzled his neck and pressed her lips against the pulse beating in his throat. "Call him back. Let's meet him and see what he has to say. We can use all the allies we can possibly get on our side."

With her soft breasts pressed against his chest and her wavy hair tickling his chin, he couldn't refuse her anything.

He sat up and reached for the phone. He put it back on Speaker and punched in the number Bessler had left.

The agent picked up on the first ring. "Yeah?"

"Bessler, I got your message."

"Duvall?" Bessler released a long, ragged sigh.

"Start talking."

"I'm in the same boat as you, man. The juice stopped working on me or something. I started remembering things, terrible things I'd done."

Max flinched and Ava ran her hand down his back.

"How did you find me? Why are you off the grid?"

"I knew you were with Dr. Whitman. I knew Dr. Whitman had a brother in Snow Haven. She told me herself that he was headed there to be a snowboard instructor. And I'm off the grid because I chucked my phone, just like you."

Max glanced at Ava and she pressed three fingers to her lips and nodded.

"I tracked her brother down, broke into his place to see if I could find out anything about Dr. Whitman. But I didn't know I'd be running straight into a Tempest trap."

"What does that mean?"

"You took him out, didn't you? The agent in the bathroom. I knew it was you as soon as I heard the circumstances. If he had seen me here, I'd be dead. I may still be dead. I can't talk any more, Duvall."

"We meet in broad daylight, tomorrow."

"In public."

"Exactly. There's an ice-skating rink in the center of town. Be there at noon in a green scarf and cap."

"And how will I know you?"

"I'll be in a green scarf and cap, too." Max drummed his fingers on the receiver. "And I have one more question for you."

"Yeah?"

"How many blue pills do you have left?"

"Not nearly enough, man, not nearly enough."

When the call ended, Ava took the phone and placed it back on the nightstand. "He sounds legitimate, doesn't he?"

"He said all the right things."

"His story makes sense, Max. I did tell him about Cody because Adrian is a snowboarder, too. He must've heard about the massacre at the lab and somehow knew I escaped. He ditched his phone to go off the grid and then figured he might find us here. It all adds up."

"I repeat—too convenient."

She stretched out on the bed, raising her arms above her head and grasping the headboard. "I believe him."

He dusted his hands together. "If you believe Agent Adrian Bessler, so do I."

"Really? That was easy."

"We'll find out if he's legit one way or the other tomorrow, and I'm not gonna lie, I care more about getting back to you than I do about Bessler because you look totally irresistible like this." He ran the flat of one hand down from her neck to her belly, and she shimmied beneath his touch.

The worry lines around her mouth and eyes dissolved, and the knots in his own gut loosened just a little. He had no idea if Bessler would try to kill him or if he'd have to take out Bessler.

It didn't matter right now. Regardless of what Bessler had to offer, he had limited time with Ava and he wasn't going to waste another minute of it discussing Tempest.

Or how he'd have to leave her in two days to protect her from the inevitable rage that would take over his mind and body.

She wiggled her toes. "We still need to eat dinner, but I'm all for room service in bed."

"With reality TV?" He flipped open the room service menu.

"What else?"

They ordered cheeseburgers and French fries and chocolate cake and spent the evening in bed eating and talking and laughing. And he'd never felt so alive.

Then he popped a blue pill, leaving one in the tin, and made love to Ava again as if it was his last night on earth.

MAX STOOD IN front of a mirror in the hotel's ski shop and wrapped the scarf around his neck. "Why did I pick green?"

"Probably because it stands out in the crowd." She adjusted the ends of his scarf and patted his chest.

"It stands out in the crowd because nobody wears it." The matching hat Ava held in her hands brought out the emerald color of her eyes, and he knew why he'd chosen the color—he'd been thinking about her eyes.

He took the hat from her and pulled it onto his head. "Bessler will definitely be able to pick me out."

"And you him, but wait for the signal from me first. If I see him at the skating rink and he's not wearing green, that's a sure sign he's planning to ambush you."

"He could just be the lure with someone else waiting there to ambush me. That's why you stay out of sight and keep your distance from me."

"Got it."

He swept the cap from his head and yanked the scarf from his neck. "I guess these will do."

He paid for the hat and scarf and took Ava's hand as they walked out of the store. "Are you hungry? You hardly touched your breakfast."

"I'm too nervous to eat. I hope…" She lifted her shoulders and then dropped them.

"You hope what?" He brought her hand to his lips and kissed each knuckle, one by one.

"I don't know. I just hope Adrian has a plan,

that he's discovered something we haven't." Her green eyes sparkled with tears. "You have one pill left, Max."

"I know that, Ava."

She rounded on him and dug her fingers into his shoulder. "What do you plan to do when it's gone?"

"I'm not going to subject you to another Simon. I'm not going to subject anyone to that."

She bit her lip and one tear trembled on the edge of her long lashes. "We can get you help."

"A padded cell?" He shook his head. "T-101 is not exactly an FDA-approved drug. No doctor is going to know what to do with me, and they won't have a chance to even experiment. Tempest wouldn't allow that."

"What about the CIA? Prospero?"

"I told you, Ava." He caught the tear on the end of his thumb. "I don't know who I can trust, except you. I trust you."

She stared past him bleakly, her eyes dead. "I love you, Max."

The words rushed over him in a warm wave, and he closed his eyes to savor every sensation those words inspired. With Ava's faith in him, he'd achieved a monumental goal. Caring for her, loving her had made him human—more human than any antidote.

He kissed her right there in the hallway outside the ski shop. "I love you, too, Dr. Whitman. Now let's get some coffee or hot chocolate and get ready to skate."

In the coffee shop, Max planted his elbows on the little table between them, hunching forward. "What do you remember about Bessler?"

"He's husky, blond, usually has a buzz cut." She skimmed her finger through the mountain of whipped cream floating on her cocoa and sucked it into her mouth.

He dragged his gaze away from her lips. He had to stay focused on this meeting with Bessler. "I don't mean his physical appearance. What was he like? Seems like he was one of the talkers if he told you he was a snowboarder and you mentioned your brother to him."

"He was nice, young." She snapped her fingers. "He was like you and Simon—friendly, talkative. A lot of the guys were reticent, didn't have much to say for themselves."

"So, you think Bessler could be on the up-and-up because he was friendly?"

"It kind of makes sense, or at least it's a positive sign. You three were not affected by the T-101 as much as the others." She sipped her hot chocolate and ended up with a fluff of whipped cream on her nose.

He reached over and dabbed it off. "Would you stop doing all that with the whipped cream?"

"Doing what?" She rubbed the back of her hand across the tip of her nose, her eyes widening.

"I'm supposed to be running through my plan for meeting Bessler and you're flicking whipped cream all over your body."

Her lips twitched into a smile. "You need to get your mind out of the gutter."

"It's not the gutter I'm imagining." He drew a line with his fingertip from her slender throat down to the V of her sweater. "It's a big bed with tousled covers and tousled hair and lots of whipped cream."

She swallowed and whispered, "Maybe if everything goes well with Bessler, we'll have time to live out that fantasy."

It always came back to that. She had to stop dreaming. He had one blue pill left, one pill between him and sure madness. And he planned to be as far away from Ava as possible when that madness descended.

"Hmm, don't know about that." He rolled his eyes to the ceiling.

"Wh-what? I have faith."

"I don't know if I want whipped cream or warm fudge and strawberries—maybe both, maybe all three."

Blinking her eyes, she smiled through her

sniffles. "Once we get out of this mess, you can have me any way you want me."

He smacked the table. "You just pumped up my motivation tenfold."

She tapped her phone. "It's time. It's eleven forty-five."

"So it is."

They left their cups on a tray and made their way to the front of the hotel for the lunchtime shuttle into town. A few other guests from the hotel joined them, and then the driver hopped in.

He looked in his rearview mirror and called out, "This shuttle is going into town, makes one stop and then turns around."

The driver cranked the doors shut, and the bus lurched forward.

Max closed his eyes, trying to visualize his meeting with Bessler, but instead of a green scarf, all he saw was a pair of sparkling green eyes, and the thought kept pounding his brain that this could be his last day with Ava.

Even if Bessler hadn't called to lure him out and kill him, the other agent probably didn't have much to offer and he hadn't had Ava to help him. Bessler had called out for help—not much chance he could solve the problem.

The shuttle turned the corner and threw Ava against his shoulder. She stayed put, and Max draped his arm across the back of her seat and drummed his fingers on her collarbone.

She'd put on a good face today, but she'd been tense and had seemed on the verge of tears a couple of times. He'd take the coward's way out and slip away in the middle of the night. Ironic for a man who'd been searching for human emotion for the past two years only to escape from it in the end.

She pointed past his shoulder at the yellow tape tied to a post near the restrooms and waving in the breeze. "The bathroom isn't cordoned off, so it's obviously not a crime scene."

"Obviously. I heard a man dropped dead of a heart attack in there."

"This time it will be different." She laced her fingers through his and kissed the back of his hand.

He put his lips close to her ear. "Remember, we part company when we get off the shuttle. Head to the skating rink via the main drag, and I'll slip through the backstreets."

She nodded.

"If you don't see Bessler at all or you see him and he's not wearing green, just send me the text we agreed upon."

"No green."

"I'm gonna make a spy out of you yet." He pinched her soft earlobe. "We give him fifteen minutes to show. Then you return to the restaurant where we had lunch with Cody."

"Holly's. If he's there and wearing green, I'll text you *green*."

"And the most important part of the plan?"

"I stay out of Bessler's sight, keep out of the open and stick with other people."

"You got it." The bus rumbled to a stop and the doors, front and back, creaked open.

"Have a great day, folks. The shuttles are still running on a reduced schedule, so we'll just have five more runs with the last one at two o'clock, and then we start up again for dinner at five."

Ava stood up first. She leaned over and kissed him on the lips. "Good luck."

She was the only luck he needed.

He brushed a knuckle across her cheek. "Be careful."

He watched her hop off the bus and tag along behind a couple on their way to the main street.

"Sir, are you getting off or going back to the hotel?"

"Just looking for my hat." He plucked it from his lap and pulled it over his head. "Found it."

He jumped onto the sidewalk, still wet from the rain the night before, but not icy. He slipped around the corner of the bathroom, wondering if the Tempest cleanup crew had ever found Snyder's weapon.

With his muscles tense and all his senses on high alert, he navigated the backstreets of Snow Haven, which was neither snowy nor a haven for anything but traps. Total fail on that name.

He reached an alley between two buildings that led to the town square at the end of the main street. On one end of that square was the ice-skating rink, which abutted the end of a ski run. That town run hadn't yet opened for the season, and brown patches and clumps of trees dotted the side of the hill.

Reaching the end of the alley, he poked his head out and looked down the sidewalk both ways. The crowds of people that would usually clog the streets during the full ski season were thinned out, but enough people milled around the shops and restaurants to give him some cover.

He let out a breath and leaned against the wall, pulling his phone from his jacket pocket where he cupped it in his palm. A chill seeped through his veins as his adrenaline merged with the T-101 still pumping through his system.

He recognized the feeling. He welcomed it.

The phone buzzed in his hand and he glanced at the display. He read the one word aloud as if to connect him with Ava. "'Green.'"

Game time.

Squaring his shoulders, he pushed off the wall and stepped onto the sidewalk, his gaze sweeping the town square. He joined a clutch of people heading for the skating rink as he hunched his shoulders and pulled his scarf around his face.

He spotted Bessler immediately hanging over the side of the rink, watching the skaters, his green scarf tucked into a black jacket. What else did he have tucked in there?

Max waited in line at the booth and then paid to rent a pair of ice skates and for an afternoon of ice-skating. He picked out a pair of skates and slung them over his shoulder.

Bessler had raised his head and was staring across the rink. He'd been made, but did Bessler have to be so obvious? Ava was right. The other agent was young and green—another good reason for the chosen color.

Max stalked toward the skating rink, waiting for Bessler to make his move. The agent clumped toward the opening of the circular rink and glided onto the ice. At least the guy could ice-skate.

Max edged around to a less populated rim and gripped the wooden railing that circled the ice. He smiled and waved to a little girl, hanging on to her mother's hand and wobbling across the ice. Maybe her mother would have him arrested before he could even talk to Bessler.

Bessler skimmed around the ice, even doing a few turns and jumps. Then he started making wide circles around the perimeter of the rink, stopping every few laps to watch the rest of the action.

He neared Max and then bent over to adjust his laces. He came to a stop a few feet away from Max.

Max leaned forward and waved again. "How'd you know where we were staying?"

Bessler replied to the ice, his head still bent. "I bugged Dr. Whitman's brother's place. I heard him on the phone. Tempest doesn't know about Cody Whitman. They tracked you here some other way. Do you still have your Tempest phone?"

"Of course not." Max didn't want to reveal too much to Bessler just yet, so he didn't need to know about Arnoff's computer. "What do you know?"

"I know they're pumping us full of juice to brainwash us, to create some superagent, but it's not working on me, at least not completely. I heard Skinner went nuts and shot up the lab but Dr. Whitman escaped. I know she's with you."

"She's not with me anymore." Max laughed and waved at his imaginary daughter. "You're doing great, sweetheart."

"Cut it out, Duvall." Bessler untied his laces again. "I heard a lot more from Cody Whitman than where you two were staying. He's trying to find a lab for you. Why?"

Max whistled between his teeth. He had to

admit the guy had skills. "How do I know this isn't a setup?"

"If it were, you'd be dead by now."

"Or you would. Don't flatter yourself, kid." A woman barreled into the side of the rink, almost tripping over Bessler.

Catching her arm, Max said, "Be careful."

"I don't think this is my thing." She laughed and then skated off.

Max leaned back and looked over his shoulder. "Besides, I don't think Tempest wants to kill me. Snyder already had his chance."

"Snyder?" Bessler finished tying his skate and brushed ice chips from his snow pants.

"The guy in the bathroom."

"Why does Dr. Whitman need the lab, Duvall? Can she create more of the juice? A weaker strain like the blue pills? Because that's one thing I do know. We can't quit cold turkey or we'll wind up like Skinner—and I have no intention of winding up like Skinner."

Bessler rose from his crouch and then his blue eyes widened as he clapped the side of his neck.

Max dropped to the ground and hugged the ice rink's barrier. He didn't need to see it—he'd heard it.

Bessler crashed to the ice.

Chapter Sixteen

Adrian Bessler fell to the ice and Ava stifled a scream when Max disappeared behind the ice rink's barrier. They'd both been hit.

She dropped the cup of hot chocolate she'd been drinking on the ground and rushed toward the ice rink, her heart pounding, her mouth dry.

A few people had stopped next to Bessler, but nobody had panicked yet. Did they think he'd just fallen? Wasn't there any blood? And why had nobody gone to Max's aid on the other side of the barrier?

She ran onto the ice, her booted feet slipping beneath her. Five feet away from Bessler, she fell, her hands hitting the cold, solid surface. Sobbing, she crawled toward the fallen agent on her hands and knees.

He looked as though he was sleeping. There was no blood on the ice, no gaping wound in his head.

"Is he your husband? I think he might've fallen and hit his head. He's out."

Ava gazed past the woman's blurry face to the place where Max had just been standing. Had nobody on the other side of the wall seen him go down?

As she dragged herself toward Bessler's inert form, attracting more and more attention, Max's head popped up on the other side of the barrier.

"What the hell are you doing?"

She nearly collapsed to the ice in relief. "I—I thought…"

"Doesn't matter what you thought. Stand up and do it quickly. I'm going to yank you over this wall."

The eyes of the woman attending to Bessler bulged from their sockets as they ping-ponged between her and Max.

An attendant in a blue parka started skating toward them.

"Wait!" Ava grabbed the lapels of Bessler's jacket. "His pills."

The Good Samaritan sat back on her heels. "Oh, does he have a heart condition?"

"Yes, yes."

Max growled. "Let's go."

Ignoring his command, Ava unzipped Bessler's jacket and patted his pocket, her hands tracing over his weapon. In a tiny inner zippered pocket, she felt the outlines of a pill bottle. With trembling fingers, she unzipped the pocket and snatched the pill bottle.

"You need to get off that ice—now."

The attendant skated up. "What happened? Does he need an ambulance?"

"He might have had a heart attack." The woman pointed to Ava, now crawling across the ice toward Max behind the wall. "His wife was looking for his pills."

"Ma'am?"

Ava twisted her head over her shoulder. "I'm not his wife. I've never seen this man before in my life."

When she reached the barrier, Max leaned over and pulled her over the wall. She landed on top of him.

"Stupid, stupid thing to do." He pinned her against the wall, clamping his hands on her shoulders. "Stay down and keep to the wall."

Bending forward, they edged along the wooden barrier, as the buzz on the ice grew. Was Bessler dead? Why had he gone down? "Max…"

"Shh. We're going out the front way. I think they hit him from behind the rink, from the mountainside."

He whipped off his hat and shed his scarf. "Take off that jacket in case they saw you."

She shrugged off her jacket, shoving the pill bottle in the front pocket of her jeans.

Max grabbed her hand and pulled her behind the rental booth. "We can't sit around and wait for the shuttle. I saw some taxis by the ski rental shop back toward the bus stop."

They weaved up and down a few streets, sidling along the walls of buildings, joining groups of pedestrians on the sidewalk. They meandered through the ski shop and exited on the other side.

Max hailed the first taxi he saw. He bundled Ava into the backseat and said, "Snow Haven Lodge and Resort."

Bessler's bottle was radiating heat in her pocket and it took all her self-control not to dig it out and discover its contents.

When the taxi reached the hotel, they marched through the lobby without speaking one word. Finally, when Max slammed the door of their suite behind him, she pulled out the bottle.

He took a turn around the room, raking a hand through his hair. "What were you thinking? You were supposed to stay out of sight—no matter what."

"I thought you'd been hit. I saw Bessler go down and almost at the same time you went down, too."

"Doesn't matter."

"It does matter. Nothing else matters." She

flipped off the lid of the bottle and peered inside. Her heart did a somersault in her chest. "Look, Max."

He stopped pacing and pivoted. "What?"

She dumped the blue pills into her palm and held out her hand. "Two of them. We have two more days together."

Her smile faded as she studied his face, his jaw hardening, the lines deepening. "I-it's two more days, Max."

His harsh laugh frightened her.

"Is that how I'm supposed to measure out my days left on earth? By counting little blue pills?"

She closed her hand around the pills and dropped her lashes. "These represent two days we didn't have before."

"It doesn't make any difference, Ava. Are we going to lure other Tempest agents here, get them killed and steal their stash?"

Anger flashed across her chest. "That's not how it happened. I'm sorry for Adrian, but he found us. I just took advantage of a terrible situation. Does that make me selfish? Then, yes, call me selfish for wanting to spend another two days with the man I love, the man I can't live without."

He reached her in two long steps and crushed her against his body. He buried his face in her hair. "You have to, Ava. You have to go on without me."

She clung to him, tears stinging her eyes. "I have the formula for the antidote, Max. I can save you."

"And what lab, what hospital is going to allow you to mix it up?" He drew back from her, cupping her face in his large hands, strands of her hair still clinging to his beard.

"A lab at the CIA or Prospero. They're the good guys. They'll help you."

"They've also put their trust in Tempest. Don't you think Tempest has already put out the word? Rogue agents, armed and dangerous. If the CIA doesn't kill me first, they'll send me back to Tempest to deprogram. I'm an intelligence asset. They can't allow me to walk the streets spouting crazy conspiracy theories."

"And Prospero?"

Furrows creased his brow. "I don't know. They're a wild card. Why did Tempest's leader choose that name and moniker of Caliban for himself?"

"You said it yourself. Tempest is the dark side of Prospero. Where Prospero is a force for good, Tempest is a force for evil."

"That's just it. Is Tempest the flip side of Prospero? Two sides of the same coin? I can't take that chance. I'm not going to end up in Tempest's clutches again."

"Caliban doesn't want to kill you, does he?"

He released her and fell across the bed, toeing off his shoes. "Do you know what happened to Bessler?"

"No." She sat on the foot of the bed. "He wasn't shot. There was no blood."

"Someone shot him in the neck with a tranquilizer dart."

"Do you think he's dead?"

"I don't know, but the same type of attack was planned for me and I know my dose wouldn't have been lethal. I would've wound up in the hospital, and my helpful brother or doctor or even wife would've come to collect me, bearing all the necessary ID and paperwork to airlift me to a facility of their choosing."

"They're diabolical."

"To say the least." He punched a pillow. "Tempest wants me back, but I'm not playing along. Before I'd go back to my so-called life at Tempest, I'd rather…"

Her nose tingled and she gulped back a sob. He'd rather kill himself. And what could she do to stop him? He didn't want to be around her once the withdrawal from the T-101 turned him into a raging machine.

She shivered as she recalled Simon Skinner's

dead eyes through the glass at the lab. She never wanted to look into Max's deep, dark eyes and see that look. Better to remember the warmth kindling there as he made love to her.

She'd have that memory forever, and she'd never let it go.

Opening her hand, she stretched it out toward him. "We still have three more days. Let me have those three last days with you."

He pinched the two pills between his thumb and forefinger, took the tin from his pocket and dropped them inside to join the other. "We'll make these three days feel like an eternity."

She scooted between his legs and rested against his chest, feeling at home against the steady beat of his heart. "Let's start now."

He stroked her hair. "God, I was so terrified when I saw you on the ice, I didn't even ask if you were okay. *Are* you okay?"

"I'll probably have a couple of bruises on my knees. I'm sorry that I tore out there like an idiot, but you disappeared right after I saw Adrian collapse. I thought they'd gotten to you, too."

"I have no doubt they planned to nail both of us, but I think they wanted to get me first. Bessler stood up suddenly and that's when he was hit. I knew immediately what had happened, so I dropped."

She ran a hand along his belly. "I'm glad I did

go out there. I remembered he'd said something about not having enough blue pills, so I figured he must've had a couple. And he did."

"Poor kid. I kind of have to believe now that he was on the up-and-up, unless Caliban plans to kill him to tie up a loose end."

"What else did he say before he was hit?"

"I'd forgotten all about what he said, but it was interesting." He toyed with her fingers. "He's the one who broke into your brother's place, and he bugged it. That's how he knew we were staying here, and he knew your brother was trying to secure a lab for us."

"That's two pieces of good news." She balanced her chin on his chest. "Maybe Tempest doesn't know about Cody. They tracked us here through Dr. Arnoff's computer, and so far they don't know we're holed up here."

"And the second thing?"

"That my brother was actually trying to find a lab for us."

"You doubted that?"

"He's my brother. I know him too well." She shifted to Max's side and twined her leg through his. "Did you tell Bessler why we needed the lab?"

"No. I didn't trust him until the moment he got shot with the dart. I still don't trust him, but he figured you might be mixing up a batch of weak T-101 to get us through the withdrawals."

"Adrian was sharp. He removed himself from Tempest's tracking system and managed to find us faster than Tempest did." She sighed. "What a waste."

"At this rate, Tempest isn't going to have any agents left to do its dirty work."

"He'll recruit more, won't he? Caliban. This whole thing—" she fashioned a big circle in the air with her hands "—is bigger than you and me. It's not just about developing an antidote to T-101. It's about stopping Caliban."

"We have to find out who he is before anyone can stop him."

"Do you really believe the CIA and Prospero are in league with him? It seems to me they're the two agencies that *can* stop him."

He ruffled her hair. "That's for you to find out, Ava. You're going to see this thing through. I have faith in you."

She clenched her teeth and pushed the dark feelings aside. When she and Max were lying here together, so close both physically and mentally, she could forget that they had just three more days together before he left her. And she'd never see him again.

He must've sensed her funk because he curled his toes against her feet and nuzzled her neck.

"We picked at breakfast and skipped lunch completely. Are you down with another feast in bed?"

"I could go for that." She twisted her fingers together. "What's going to happen to Bessler?"

"If he's still alive, Tempest probably has him. If he's dead, the cleanup crew will take care of all the details."

"I'd like to think he's alive. Tempest can have him for now, but when I produce that antidote we'll get him back." She sat up, her heart galloping. "That's it, Max."

"Hmm?" He looked up from the room service menu and she snatched it from his hands.

"Tempest can have you back, too. Eventually, I'll have that formula ready to go and we'll save all of the Tempest agents, including you."

One side of his mouth quirked up in a half smile. "How will you ever find me again?"

She blinked. "I'll find you, Max. Wherever you are in the world, whatever you're doing, I'll find you."

"I almost believe you when you talk like that." He rubbed his hand up her arm, and she shook him off impatiently.

"Tell me you'll think about it. We may even get the antidote to you before Tempest can send you out in the field again."

"I'll think about it." He shook open the menu

again and ran his finger down a row of items. "Cheeseburgers were good, but I could go for some pasta."

She stared at him over the edge of the menu and held her breath. It wouldn't do any good to shout at this immovable piece of granite. She'd work on him gradually. Hell, she wasn't above using her body to convince him. She'd give him such a mind-blowing experience in bed tonight, he'd agree to anything.

"You're smiling." He tapped her with the corner of the menu. "I see you like the idea of pasta."

"Let me see that thing." She held out her hand for the menu. "Do they have any whipped cream, hot fudge and strawberries?"

He raised an eyebrow at her. "I don't know what the strawberries would be like this time of year, but I'm sure they can scrape up some hot fudge and whipped cream."

"Purrrfect." She arched her back and tousled her hair.

He grabbed her around the waist and pulled her into his arms. "You're damned sexy, Dr. Whitman."

She wouldn't even correct him this time. He could call her Dr. Whitman until his dying day, as long as he delayed his dying day by turning himself over to Tempest.

Closing her eyes, she lifted her face for his kiss. When it didn't come, she opened one eye to find Max searching her face.

She thrust out her bottom lip. "What happened to that kiss?"

"You are so beautiful." His fingers dabbled lightly over her nose and mouth. "I'm imprinting you on my memory."

"You're already imprinted here in my heart." She tapped her chest, tight with emotion.

He tossed the menu over his shoulder. "It's a little early for dinner anyway. I think I want my dessert first—forget the whipped cream."

Just when they got comfortable under the covers, her phone rang. As always these days, the sound caused a shaft of fear to plow through her heart.

She rolled to the side and swept it from the nightstand. She met Max's eyes over the glowing display and peeled her tongue from the roof of her mouth. "It's Cody."

"Answer it."

"What's up, Cody? Are you okay?"

"Besides a string of crazy things happening in Snow Haven ever since you and that cyborg showed up, I'm fine. And you're gonna be fine, too."

"Why? What happened?"

"I got you a lab."

Chapter Seventeen

"Where? How? What?" She bounced on the bed. "I love you. You're the best brother in the world."

"Wow, before I was the scourge of mankind for mixing you up in my illegal activities. Now I'm freakin' hero material."

"Cut to the chase, Cody." Max threw off the covers and swung his legs over the side of the bed.

"You could've told me I was on Speaker, Ava." Cody coughed. "Hey, man, I totally meant that cyborg comment as a compliment."

Max grunted. "Whatever. Spill."

"That one guy I knew who was out of town got back to me when he heard about the money involved. He knows I'm no snitch."

"Which is coming in very handy right now." Ava's voice squeaked. She could barely contain her excitement. "Go on."

"Anyway, he has a place that he abandoned because the DEA was onto him."

Max interrupted. "Does the DEA know about this place?"

"No. My friend abandoned the place when the DEA started tailing him. Nobody knows about the lab except him and his partner, and now us."

Max asked, "Where's his partner?"

"Uh, dude's in jail."

"Great." Ava nibbled the side of her thumb. "Where is this place, Cody? Is it ready to go?"

"I already have the key and the code and someone's delivering all the chemicals you need as we speak. I gave the guy your money already, including the dude who got the chemicals, and I kept my cut. You said I could keep a percentage, right?"

"We did." Max walked to the window and peered through the blinds. "How are we going to get the key from you? I don't want you near the hotel right now."

"I don't think I'm being followed. Haven't noticed anything since the break-in."

"Humor the cyborg."

Cody choked. "A friend of mine works at the Haven Brewery in town. Her name's Dina. I'll leave it with her—no questions asked."

"Got it." Max grabbed the hotel pad of paper by the phone. "Now, where is this lab?"

Cody gave them detailed directions to a place south of Salt Lake City, along with the code for the door. "You have to follow these directions exactly because you'll never find the place using your GPS or a map. As far as I can tell, it's in the middle of nowhere."

"That's exactly what we're looking for." Ava took a twirl around the room. "Cody?"

"Yeah?"

"Have I ever told you you're the best brother in the world?"

"Yeah, like five minutes ago. Look, I don't know what you two are up to, but be careful. And, cyborg?"

"Are you talking to me?" Max rolled his eyes at Ava.

"Don't let anything bad happen to my sister. She's all I got."

"I won't." Max joined her at the foot of the bed and curled his arm around her shoulders, pulling her close. "She's all I got, too."

When Cody hung up, Ava jumped into Max's arms, wrapping her legs around his waist. "He came through. I can't believe it. He came through."

"Are you sure you want to do this?" He smoothed her hair back from her face. "It's going to be dangerous."

She wrinkled her nose. "How? I've been working in labs for the past ten years of my life. I know my way around a lab."

"Adrian Bessler had your brother bugged. How do we know Tempest hasn't done the same?"

"You said yourself, Tempest tracked us here from Arnoff's computer. Tempest doesn't know about Cody. He's off their radar."

"He was, but nothing remains a secret from Tempest for long."

"Then we'd better get moving." She wriggled out of his arms. "I've got a batch of T-101 antidote to cook up."

"Before we start packing up—" he shook his tin of pills "—I'm going to pop one of these for what I hope is my last time."

A half an hour later, they'd packed their bags and Ava stood at the door looking back into the room.

Max nudged her. "Are you ready?"

"I just want to remember where I spent one of the happiest nights of my life."

He kissed her ear. "I'm going to give you plenty of those, Dr. Whitman."

With the car packed up, they drove into town and parked in a public lot. Max hesitated before opening the door.

"What's wrong?"

"Every time we come into this town, something bad happens."

Before she opened her door, she blew him a kiss. "Our luck just changed."

The crowds on the streets of Snow Haven were thicker at night than during the day, the restaurants bustling with people eagerly awaiting the first snowfall.

The Haven Brewery had a line out the door, and Max shouldered his way through, dragging her along in his wake.

They hung on the end of the bar, and Ava tapped the wrist of a waitress picking up a tray of drinks. "Is Dina here tonight?"

She pointed to a pretty blonde behind the bar, filling a pitcher of beer. "Dina! Customer over here wants to see you."

Ava thanked the waitress, and when Dina finished topping off the pitcher, she wiped her hands on a bar towel and approached them.

"Let's see, you want the Haven pale ale and you want the Haven IPA, right?" She winked.

Ava nodded, suppressing a smile. Cody couldn't resist going all secret agent on them.

When Dina slid the beers toward them, she slipped a key beneath Ava's mug.

Ava took a sip of beer through the foam, the malty taste filling her mouth. "This is good."

Max eyed her over the rim of his mug. "Do you really think you should be tipsy in the lab?"

"It's one beer."

"One very big beer, and I've already seen how you handle your booze, and it ain't pretty."

She punched his rock-hard biceps and took another tiny sip of beer. Her ears perked up when she heard the man next to them mention the ice-skating rink.

She glanced at Max, but she could tell by the hard lines of his face that he was already focused on the conversation.

"Yeah, it was weird. The guy went down like a sack of potatoes. I guess he tripped or something, but he wasn't getting up."

Max sidled closer to the man and said, "I was there watching my daughter skate. We left when he was still down. What happened to him? Did he die?"

The man took a gulp of his beer and wiped the foam from his upper lip. "No, no, that was the other guy in the bus station bathroom. That guy dropped dead from a heart attack, I heard. This guy was okay."

"Really?" Ava gripped the handle of her mug so hard, she half expected it to explode in her hand. "You mean he got up and skated away?"

"Nah, some guy, a family member I guess, came to his rescue and got him up."

Max traced a bead of moisture on the outside of his glass. "The attendant was going to call 911. Did the ambulance take him away?"

"Nope. His brother, or whatever, took him away before the ambulance got there." He elbowed his friend in the ribs. "Some brother. If it was me, I'd want to go to the hospital. That guy was out cold, from the looks of it."

"Yeah, me too." Max shoved his glass away from him. "We gotta go, honey. Olive will be happy to hear the man at the rink was okay."

Ava waved to Dina and pushed back from the bar.

Max paid for the drinks, leaving Dina a hundred-dollar tip.

When they hit the sidewalk, Max cursed and took her arm, hustling her toward the parking lot.

"What's wrong, Max? I know you think being in Tempest's clutches is the worst thing ever, but at least Adrian's alive."

"Being a Tempest drone is not being alive, Ava."

She puffed out a breath, happy for the hundredth time that Cody had secured the lab. Max would've never gone for her plan to return to Tempest only to be rescued by the antidote later, no matter how much whipped cream and hot fudge were involved.

He beeped the remote for their little car. "It's not just being under the spell of Tempest again. Tempest has Bessler and they'll be privy to any information he has—including info about Cody and maybe even the bug Bessler put in his place. Do you know if Cody was home when he called us?"

Max's words had instilled a cold fear throughout her body. "I think so. We need to warn him."

"I don't want you to call him. If Tempest does know about him, he'll be tracked."

She pressed a fist to her lips and then clapped her hands. "Dina! I'll give a message to him via Dina. She's already proven herself to be discreet."

"I'll drive you around the front of the bar and wait for you in the street."

He exited the parking lot and pulled the car in front of the bar, double-parking.

Ava ran into the bar, threading her way through the crowd. She gestured to Dina to join her at the end of the bar.

"Hey, thanks for the tip."

"Do you want another?"

The girl's heavily lined eyes widened. "Sure."

"I need to get a message to Cody but I can't call him on his phone. I don't want you to call him with this message either. Can you get him to come down here and talk to him in person?"

She smiled a slow, seductive smile. "I can get Cody to do anything I want."

"Too much information." Ava held up her hand. "When he gets here, tell him to leave town immediately and throw his phone away. Tell him it's life-and-death."

Dina's jaw dropped. "Seriously?"

"Seriously."

"I'll do it, of course."

"Thanks." Ava slipped her another hundred-dollar bill, courtesy of Max's stash. "Maybe you should join him."

She ran back to the car, still double-parked, and jumped in. "Done."

"We need to get out to that lab as soon as possible."

They left town just as a light snow began dusting the treetops. Max maneuvered the car down the mountain and they sped past Salt Lake City, heading south.

Ava clutched the piece of paper with the directions to the lab in her lap, crinkling the corners. "We're turning off in about four miles. What's the odometer reading?"

He poked a finger at the control panel. "I just reset it. I'll keep my eye on it, not that it looks like there are going to be a lot of options for turning off in the next five miles."

Darkness had descended and the snow had turned to slush.

Ava turned up the heat and folded her arms across her body. "Too warm for you?"

"It's fine." He flipped down the vent. "We

don't have to go through with this, Ava. We can drive on by and spend our last few days together someplace warm and safe."

"It's right within our reach." Her fingers danced along his forearm. "I'm not afraid."

"I know you're not. That's what scares me."

He took the turnoff and she continued to guide him by reading the directions from the notepaper. "I hope you have a flashlight in your bag of tricks because it's dark out here."

"What would you expect from a covert meth lab?" He scratched his chin. "Where did your brother get all those chemicals?"

"Don't ask." She turned in her seat. "You're not going to snitch him off, are you? I mean, about the meth lab and the drugs."

"I don't like the idea of someone out here making and selling illegal drugs, but I think under the circumstances I can let it pass." He shrugged. "Besides, the guy's out of business and his partner's in prison, right?"

"For now."

"That's all I have—right now."

He turned the car down what looked like an abandoned road, and a few buildings crouched together in a semicircle.

He cut the headlights. "Looks like there was a little light industry here at one point that never got off the ground."

She waved the paper. "It's the building on the left. It should have a keypad for the code he gave us and a padlock on the sliding door."

Max wheeled the car behind the building and parked. He dragged his bag out of the trunk and fished through it for a flashlight. He aimed the beam at the ground. "Stay close."

She hooked her finger in his belt loop and followed him around to the front of the building. As he shined the light on the keypad, she punched in the code with stiff fingers. Something clicked and she whispered, "That's a good sign."

Max inserted the key in the lock and sprang it open. He pocketed the lock. Then he yanked on the sliding door, and after a brief resistance, it slid open.

They stepped inside what felt like a cavernous space, and Max shut the door behind them.

Ava felt for the switch next to the door, and when she flipped it, white light bathed the room. She let out a long breath as she took in the gleaming stainless-steel surfaces and the neat placement of the lab equipment.

Max dropped his bag on the floor. "Wow, our meth cooker was a neat freak."

"It's perfect." She flexed her fingers. "I can do this, Max."

"Get to it." He gestured around the room. "I'm going to take care of security."

He watched Ava for a few minutes as she washed her hands, pulled on a pair of gloves and positioned a pair of safety goggles over her face. How the hell did he get so lucky to have this incredible, brave woman on his side?

He withdrew his weapon and loaded a second one. He placed it on the counter near Ava. "This one's for you. All you have to do is point and shoot."

She tapped a metal drum on the floor. "Can you crank this open for me?"

"Should I put on some gloves?"

"Yes, and some goggles. The fumes can sting your eyes."

"And you're going to be injecting me with this stuff?"

"It's better than the other stuff I'd been injecting you with for almost two years."

He opened the spigot on the drum for her. "Is this chemical flammable?"

She pointed across the room. "That stuff is. Why?"

He winked. "You do your thing, and I'll do mine."

While Ava continued to measure, pour, stir and heat, he secured the lab with a few booby traps using the equipment from his duffel. Tempest agents were always prepared.

If Tempest had their hands on Bessler, it was

only a matter of time before they got information from him on Cody, including audio from the bug Bessler had set up in Cody's apartment. They should have some time on their side, since Bessler had been completely out of it.

Once Max outfitted the room, he slid open the front door. "I'm going to move the car away from the building. Be right back."

She said something unintelligible but didn't look up from her work, so he figured it wasn't important. Once outside, he surveyed the building and couldn't detect any light coming from it.

He moved the car another twenty feet from the structure, lining it up with a boarded window in the back—their escape hatch.

He returned to the lab and punched in the code to lock the door. He sat on a table facing the door. The building had no windows, so he couldn't see anyone coming but he could hear them.

"How are you doing over there?"

"It's coming along. Say what you will about Dr. Arnoff, but the man was a genius."

"Yeah, like a mad scientist."

"This formula is beautifully simple."

"I'll take your word for it. Let's just hope after all this hoopla, the damned stuff works."

"Count on it."

He let her work in peace, his muscles aching

with the tension of the wait. Different noises came from the various equipment Ava was using, and then Max heard a low droning sound.

Tilting his head, he moved closer to Ava's work space. "What is that?"

She flipped the switch of some vibrating machine and the buzzing merged with the low drone.

He drew his finger across his throat, and she stopped the machine. "What?"

"Do you hear that noise? Is that something you're doing?"

She spread her gloved hands. "No."

Suddenly the drone turned into a roar, and the building shook.

Max clutched his weapon and tilted his head back to look at the ceiling, which seemed to be vibrating.

A voice boomed over a loudspeaker above them. "Give it up, Duvall. Come out with your hands up or we'll destroy that lab and every-thing…and everyone in it."

Chapter Eighteen

Ava dropped something on the floor and it shattered.

His heart jumped. "You okay?"

"Yeah. What do we do?"

"I'm not surrendering to Tempest, not now, not ever." He kept his weapon trained on the ceiling. "Get your stuff together. We're out of here."

"How are we going to escape? There's a helicopter up there, and I'm pretty sure they have weapons—lots of them. Besides, I..."

He held up his hand. "I know you're not ready yet, Ava, but I don't want to hear it. You have to abandon the antidote. Put down the test tube and pick up the gun I gave you."

The voice came through the bullhorn again. "We want to hear what you have to say, Duvall. Call the hotline. We'll pick up from the chopper."

Max reached for his phone, and Ava jerked her head up from pulling off her gloves. "What are you doing?"

"Buying time. I need to set our escape in motion, but I need you to pick up that gun and crouch down in the corner by the front door. Keep your goggles on."

He punched in the number for the Tempest hotline, the line they used when they got into trouble. He'd never had to use it yet.

They must've patched the line through to the helicopter because someone picked up on the first ring and it was the same voice from the loudspeaker.

"That's better, Duvall."

"Who is this? Foster?"

"Does it matter? I'm Tempest. I'm authorized to speak for Caliban."

"What do you want from me?" Max put the phone on Speaker and then crept to the boarded-up window in the back of the building, past Ava's work area, where she'd been minutes away from saving his life.

The anonymous voice continued. "We don't want to kill you, Duvall. You're a valuable asset. Caliban thinks you're the most valuable agent we have. Give yourself up to us and we'll make sure Dr. Whitman gets out of here alive."

Liars. He checked the wires he'd set up earlier and glanced at Ava huddled in the corner, one hand shoved into the pocket of her jacket, the other clutching a gun.

"Is Dr. Whitman listening?"

"Yes."

"Dr. Whitman, you can take Dr. Arnoff's place. He neglected to tell us about that antidote. We'll allow you to mix up that antidote and more closely monitor our agents, including Max."

Max headed for the front of the building, with only one ear listening to the lies spewing from the phone. He checked his wiring there and lit a fuse hanging from the ceiling. There was no turning back now.

Max gave Ava a thumbs-up sign and muted the phone. He joined her in the corner and whispered, "Stay put but get ready to move through the back of the building once it blows."

Her eyes widened. "Blows?"

He put his finger to his lips and unmuted the phone.

Ava rose from her crouch and shouted into the phone in Max's hand. "Where's Agent Bessler?"

"He's safe and sound, Dr. Whitman. We treated him and he'll be fine."

"You mean he'll be a drone for Tempest."

"It's what our agents do, Dr. Whitman. Dr. Arnoff understood that and used the opportunity to conduct experiments that would've never been allowed in the medical community. You can do the same."

Max held up the phone and nodded.

Ava yelled, "No, thanks!"

Max punched in a three-digit number on his cell phone and the back of the building exploded outward, rocking the structure.

He grabbed Ava's hand. "Let's go!"

They ran toward the gaping hole in the wall in a crouch while machine gun fire sounded from above.

He pulled Ava close. "When we hit the opening, I'm going to lunge forward and I'm taking you with me. Get ready."

They stumbled through the gap, and Max launched himself forward just as the building behind them exploded. The force propelled them closer to the car, the heat intense on his back, the ends of his hair singeing.

The helicopter above them screamed and whined, and he twisted his head around to see it lurch onto its side, its spinning blades glancing the roof of the burning building.

Max dragged himself up from the ground and Ava popped up beside him.

She clambered into the driver's side and crawled across the console to the passenger seat, dropping her weapon on the floor, and he gunned the engine before he was even sitting in the driver's seat.

Another explosion burst into the night sky as the chopper plowed through the roof of the building.

Max hit the accelerator as burning debris fell around them.

Ava turned around in her seat to watch the lab collapse. From his rearview mirror, Max witnessed a ball of fire rolling toward the sky.

Not until he reached the road that connected to the main highway did he let out a long, smoky breath.

He rubbed a patch of soot from Ava's white cheek. "Are you all right? Not hurt?"

She covered her face with her hands and said through parted fingers, "When you said you were securing the building, I didn't know that meant you were booby-trapping it."

"I figured the less you knew the better. You had other things to concentrate on. I didn't want to scare you or distract you."

"How'd you know they'd be coming by helicopter? How'd you know they'd be coming at all?"

"I didn't know about the helicopter, but car or helicopter, that explosion would stop either one. And once I heard they had Bessler, I figured it was only a matter of time before they found that lab. They'd debrief Bessler or shoot him up with truth serum or torture him, but one way or another they were going to find out everything he knew about us, including that bug he put in your brother's apartment."

She ran her hands through her hair, showering bits of debris into her lap. "I hope Dina got to Cody and he made it out of Snow Haven safely."

"Once you get to a secure location, you can call him. Tempest is not done with you, but once we part company I'm sending you to Prospero. You can tell them our story. You can show them the formula for the antidote. They'll take care of you, whether they believe you or not."

"You still don't trust Prospero? You won't come with me?"

"Even if I had the time, which I don't, I wouldn't turn myself over to Prospero, but you should be okay."

"And who says you don't have the time?"

He grabbed her hand and circled his thumb in her palm. "We're not going to find another lab and get our hands on those chemicals in three days, Ava. It was a good try and we were close. I appreciate everything you did. I more than appreciate you. I love you. Always know that."

He steeled himself for more tears. It was a bittersweet victory that he was human enough now to be undone by Ava's tears.

She laughed.

He whipped his head around, but she continued to laugh, her eyes sparkling in the darkness of the car. Maybe the stress and tension had finally driven her off the deep end.

"I guess the idea of a doomed man falling in love could be funny and I'd rather see laughter than tears from you, but are you sure you're okay?"

"You're not a doomed man, Max."

"Three pills, three days."

She plunged her hand in the pocket of her jacket. She pulled it out and opened it wide, cupping a glass vial in her palm.

"Do you want to reconsider telling me you love me? This is the T-101 antidote, and you have a lifetime with me ahead of you."

Epilogue

Prospero's chief, Jack Coburn, cleared his throat over the phone. "We've been suspicious about Tempest's actions for a while, Duvall, so I'm inclined to believe your story."

Ava came up behind Max, sitting on the edge of the hotel bed, and draped her arms around his shoulders.

He captured her hand and pressed a kiss against her palm. "Do you know who Caliban is?"

"No, but we'd like to find out."

"I take it the CIA doesn't know either."

"Caliban reports to the director, just like I do, but Tempest has always been more secretive about its organization and actions."

"Now you know why."

"I repeat my offer for both you and Ms. Whitman. You can come in from the field and we'll protect you."

"It's not that I don't trust you, Coburn."

Jack Coburn interrupted him. "But you don't trust me. I understand, but to stop Tempest we need to know more about its operations. We want to debrief you."

"I get that, but we'll have to do it over a secure connection and from a safe distance. We will take you up on the offer of the new identities though, and Ava will turn over the formula for the T-101 antidote."

"That's a deal. Be careful out there and we'll keep you posted as we move forward with this investigation."

"What's next?"

"Nina Moore, Agent Skinner's fiancée. We have reason to believe she's being watched."

"Whatever you do, take care of her."

"We're on it, Duvall. You need to disappear now."

Max ended the call and reclined on the bed, pulling her down next to him. "We're done with Tempest—for now. We'll let Prospero handle them. You know, I think that's what Caliban wanted all along—some kind of face-off between Tempest and Prospero."

"Well, it looks like he's going to get his wish." She waved a hand around the hotel room. "Do we need to disappear any more than this?"

"Prospero will send us a couple of new identities. We can go even further underground."

She caressed his strong face, which had lost its hardness since he'd taken the antidote. "Can underground include a tropical paradise somewhere?"

"Absolutely." He kissed her mouth. "But we're not joining your brother and Dina in Hawaii, if that's what you're thinking."

"Hawaii?" She snapped her fingers. "We can go more exotic than Hawaii, can't we?"

"We can go wherever you want, Dr. Whitman."

She slipped her hand beneath his T-shirt and swirled her fingernails over his hard belly. "Now that you have your life back, are you sure you want to spend it with me?"

"If you can handle a cyborg for the rest of your life."

"Cyborg?" She snuggled next to his side and rested her head against his chest. "You're all man, Max Duvall, and you're all mine—forever."

* * * * *

The showdown between Prospero and Tempest is just heating up!
Look for the continuation of Carol Ericson's
BROTHERS IN ARMS: RETRIBUTION
miniseries next month when
THE PREGNANCY PLOT goes on sale.
Look for it wherever Harlequin Intrigue books and ebooks are sold!

LARGER-PRINT
BOOKS!

◆ HARLEQUIN

Presents®

GET 2 FREE LARGER-PRINT
NOVELS PLUS 2 FREE GIFTS!

PASSION
GUARANTEED
SEDUCTION

YES! Please send me 2 FREE LARGER-PRINT Harlequin Presents® novels and my 2 FREE gifts (gifts are worth about $10). After receiving them, if I don't wish to receive any more books, I can return the shipping statement marked "cancel." If I don't cancel, I will receive 6 brand-new novels every month and be billed just $5.30 per book in the U.S. or $5.74 per book in Canada. That's a saving of at least 12% off the cover price! It's quite a bargain! Shipping and handling is just 50¢ per book in the U.S. and 75¢ per book in Canada.* I understand that accepting the 2 free books and gifts places me under no obligation to buy anything. I can always return a shipment and cancel at any time. Even if I never buy another book, the two free books and gifts are mine to keep forever.

176/376 HDN GHVY

Name	(PLEASE PRINT)	
Address		Apt. #
City	State/Prov.	Zip/Postal Code

Signature (if under 18, a parent or guardian must sign)

Mail to the **Reader Service:**
IN U.S.A.: P.O. Box 1867, Buffalo, NY 14240-1867
IN CANADA: P.O. Box 609, Fort Erie, Ontario L2A 5X3

Are you a subscriber to Harlequin Presents® books
and want to receive the larger-print edition?
Call 1-800-873-8635 today or visit us at www.ReaderService.com.

* Terms and prices subject to change without notice. Prices do not include applicable taxes. Sales tax applicable in N.Y. Canadian residents will be charged applicable taxes. Offer not valid in Quebec. This offer is limited to one order per household. Not valid for current subscribers to Harlequin Presents Larger-Print books. All orders subject to credit approval. Credit or debit balances in a customer's account(s) may be offset by any other outstanding balance owed by or to the customer. Please allow 4 to 6 weeks for delivery. Offer available while quantities last.

Your Privacy—The Reader Service is committed to protecting your privacy. Our Privacy Policy is available online at www.ReaderService.com or upon request from the Reader Service.

We make a portion of our mailing list available to reputable third parties that offer products we believe may interest you. If you prefer that we not exchange your name with third parties, or if you wish to clarify or modify your communication preferences, please visit us at www.ReaderService.com/consumerchoice or write to us at Reader Service Preference Service, P.O. Box 9062, Buffalo, NY 14240-9062. Include your complete name and address.

HPLP15

LARGER-PRINT BOOKS!
GET 2 FREE LARGER-PRINT NOVELS PLUS
2 FREE GIFTS!

♦HARLEQUIN®

Romance

From the Heart, For the Heart

YES! Please send me 2 FREE LARGER-PRINT Harlequin® Romance novels and my 2 FREE gifts (gifts are worth about $10). After receiving them, if I don't wish to receive any more books, I can return the shipping statement marked "cancel." If I don't cancel, I will receive 4 brand-new novels every month and be billed just $5.09 per book in the U.S. or $5.49 per book in Canada. That's a savings of at least 15% off the cover price! It's quite a bargain! Shipping and handling is just 50¢ per book in the U.S. and 75¢ per book in Canada.* I understand that accepting the 2 free books and gifts places me under no obligation to buy anything. I can always return a shipment and cancel at any time. Even if I never buy another book, the two free books and gifts are mine to keep forever.

119/319 HDN GHWC

Name	(PLEASE PRINT)

Address	Apt. #

City	State/Prov.	Zip/Postal Code

Signature (if under 18, a parent or guardian must sign)

Mail to the **Reader Service:**
IN U.S.A.: P.O. Box 1867, Buffalo, NY 14240-1867
IN CANADA: P.O. Box 609, Fort Erie, Ontario L2A 5X3
Want to try two free books from another line?
Call 1-800-873-8635 or visit www.ReaderService.com.

* Terms and prices subject to change without notice. Prices do not include applicable taxes. Sales tax applicable in N.Y. Canadian residents will be charged applicable taxes. Offer not valid in Quebec. This offer is limited to one order per household. Not valid for current subscribers to Harlequin Romance Larger-Print books. All orders subject to credit approval. Credit or debit balances in a customer's account(s) may be offset by any other outstanding balance owed by or to the customer. Please allow 4 to 6 weeks for delivery. Offer available while quantities last.

Your Privacy—The Reader Service is committed to protecting your privacy. Our Privacy Policy is available online at www.ReaderService.com or upon request from the Reader Service.

We make a portion of our mailing list available to reputable third parties that offer products we believe may interest you. If you prefer that we not exchange your name with third parties, or if you wish to clarify or modify your communication preferences, please visit us at www.ReaderService.com/consumerchoice or write to us at Reader Service Preference Service, P.O. Box 9062, Buffalo, NY 14240-9062. Include your complete name and address.